_NIGHT TRAIN 5

CW00943896

_NIGHT TRAIN 5

___an anthology of work by students
on the Creative Writing programmes
in the School of English at the
University of Kent

___NIGHT TRAIN PRESS
___

First published in 2007 by Night Train Press
at the School of English, Rutherford College, University of Kent,
Canterbury, Kent CT2 7NX
email: english@kent.ac.uk

British Library cataloguing in publication
A CIP record for this book is available from the British Library

ISBN 978-09548332-3-7

Edited by Susan Wicks and Andrew McGuinness

Produced by Vicky Wilson
Series design by Claudia Schenk

Printed in Great Britain by The University Print Unit, University of Kent

Cover image from Large Format short film *Where the Trains used to go*
© Morten Skallerud, Camera Magica, Norway

NOTE
The distinction between 'short prose' and 'stories' in the anthology is often
only a matter of length and reflects the mode of submission: the stories
were produced at level 2 or above and submitted by teachers on their
students' behalf; the 'short prose' was sent in, as was the poetry, by students
themselves and represents all levels, from First Year to postgraduate.

_FOREWORD

With *Night Train 5* the anthology of the University of Kent's Creative Writing Programme is moving into its third edited year. I'm delighted to say that, even shared, the job of selecting is becoming ever more difficult. This year there were more submissions, particularly for the poetry section, and a larger number of them were publishable. The earlier call for work and deadlines did seem to catch more work from our younger undergraduates, and I included all I could. Some of the decisions were delicate, and I'm sure both Andrew and I had to pretend to a thicker skin than either of us in fact possesses. Several of the short prose pieces I eventually had to reject had a big 'Y' pencilled (by me) in the top corners. But in the end we did have to choose, and quality couldn't be the only criterion: subject, tone and variety were important considerations too.

I hope potential readers will see the anthology for what it is: not just a somewhat subjective 'best' extracted from a year of our students' work, but the actual tip of a very interesting iceberg, dependent on all the other work, submitted and not submitted, on peer support and tutor insights and encouragement, on a whole atmosphere of enthusiasm and active participation and enjoyment, for its visibility and light-catching qualities as it floats past.
Susan Wicks, August 2007

The full-length stories included in this anthology were selected for their expression of voice, individuality of vision and authorial prose-control. They range in setting from the domestic to the exotic, in style and substance from gritty realism to magic realism, but what impressed me most about each story was the author's ability to take me on a journey; in the process, revealing something important or interesting about the human condition. Each one has clarity of purpose, a sense of direction, and demonstrates real short-story craft: an eye for significant detail, an ear for dialogue, a feeling for character and/or situation.

The standard was very high, so it was a genuine pleasure reading every submission, though hellishly difficult selecting those for inclusion. In the end, I chose stories which surprised me, or convinced me of a universal truth, or woke me up to a fresh reality through the storytelling. Regrettably, due to limitations of space, other very good stories had to be omitted. With this in mind, congratulations should be extended to all the writers whose work it was a joy reading, whether it appears here in print or not. Such quality and individuality is testament to the fine writing going on across the board at the University of Kent.
Andrew McGuinness, August 2007

_CONTENTS

He drops from one branch to a lower one, a fall of three times his own height, and lands lightly and perfectly balanced. The branch is wide, a solid path polished by feet over many centuries. He runs to the trunk and presses against it.

Dzargs are coming. He can feel their footfalls as vibrations in the very roots of the tree. He runs a fingertip up the curve of his pointed ear, as if to sharpen his hearing, and picks up the sound of the Dzargs' drums and, faintly, their battle song.

He runs the length of the bough, to its tip, and launches himself out, reaching for the branches on the other side of the chasm. Then, from the darkness comes an arrow, bronze-tipped, black-feathered. It pierces his shoulder as he reaches the zenith of his flight, and Christophe the elf falls, without a sound, into the abyss.

'Oh, shit, shit, shit,' says Christophe the elf, assuming the form of Gary Shooter. He's lost the elf. He's lost the bloody elf. Six weeks he's had Christophe, the longest lived of any of his characters. Ever. Hours and hours of on-line time, six or seven after work, fifteen hours a day at weekends, ended in a moment. Over a frozen image of the elf – horror in his green eyes, his golden limbs splayed against the complete black of the screen – the game lists his statistics: attributes, skills and achievements. At the bottom, under the heading 'Death' it says, 'By Ghost Wolf arrow on day 327 of the Era of Rashund.'

Gary sits dumbfounded. In any other game, he would just go back to the last saved position and play again, but this is Starfalling. Here, when you fall, you don't get up again.

In the onward rush of playing the game, in the race to gain more skills and relationships with other players, to pick up spells, amulets and weapons, there was no need or time to look back, but as he sees it all laid out on the screen he realises how rich the web of Christophe's life had become. Fifty-one spells are listed, three of them level six. He had the sword of Rashund, which can only be held by one player at a time. There will be a scrum for that when Christophe's demise is announced. He has connections to seventy other characters, including the Lady Oriele. His absence will leave her open for the Ghost Wolf, Argus, who has been sniffing around this last week. It doesn't matter to Gary that Lady Oriele may be a twenty-stone fish-gutter from Grimsby; the chemistry was there, and he will miss it.

He hits escape. Christophe and the list of achievements fades.

At the same moment, there is a window-rattling boom and the room lights up – a red flash. A few months ago, when he'd been playing Counterstrike all the time, he'd have been so keyed up, he'd probably have dived under the table, but now he only flinches slightly and looks out through the open curtains at the sky.

Guy Fawkes Night. He'd fleetingly thought of going to the display at the recreation ground. If he had, he wouldn't have been on-line, and Christophe would still be alive.

In the dark of the kitchen, he opens the fridge. The fridge light glows through the golden oil separated out of the salad dressing and through the blue bottle of Bombay Sapphire. He takes a can of coke, drinks a few mouthfuls and tops it up with the gin. At the window, he watches brilliant emerald bursts in the sky. There's a rattling like tracer fire. The explosions leave after-images, smoky dandelion heads, which instantly begin to disperse, blowing eastwards.

A little girl tows her father as they run down the road, late for the display. Her stringy legs in thick tights, her oversized coat and her hat with earflaps remind Gary of his sister. He can remember her with a hat exactly like that. Now she works for an oil company in Calgary and wears Chanel suits and discreet gold jewellery. She has her sleek chestnut crop cut every week. Seventy dollars to slice away the most minuscule length of hair. She speaks to Gary less often than that, maybe once a month. In the image relayed by her webcam, she gleams, glossy and clean.

Gary rubs his stubbled chin. A shower of electric blue orbs lights up the garden. The leaves still clinging to the cherry tree turn grey and cast sharp-cut shadows. The sound is delayed by no more than a fraction of a second, but enough to make him feel strange. He stands in the window, occasionally swigging the gin and coke until the display ends and the families start pouring back up the road to reclaim cars. Kids wave glow sticks bent into circles, green as fireflies. He remembers them from raves in the nineties: Shelley dancing with that eerie fluorescence around her neck and her smile blue-white in the ultraviolet lights. Where would she be now? What would she be doing? She used to keep her glow sticks in the freezer; it made them last longer but, even so, they faded after a few days to a dull plastic tube with a faint lime tinge.

When the road's empty again, he goes back to the fridge, tops up the coke can with gin and sits down in front of the computer. He reloads Starfalling. This time he'll be a Ghost Wolf, maybe a female Ghost Wolf – a distraction for Christophe's rival, Argus, in his pursuit of the Lady Oriele. The character set-up screen loads. Name?

He types, 'Christa.'

With my steady, shuffling pace, I reached the moon much quicker than expected. I had seen it from the side of the country lane that led me out of Stonesfield that night, and had had to light a Lucky Strike, and use the smoke to shield me from its glare. I had left the path, and walked into the warm summer fields to find the moon. It hung too low in the sky, with a rare rectangular shape and sharp quality to it that tethered me to the Earth.

I hopped a moist wooden gate and walked up a gravel path to where someone had left a 60-metre tall tower crane in the middle of a field. It was a dark burgundy red, barely visible in the night, apart from the rectangle moon that was held at its peak. The moon looked like a sign, maybe the place where they would write the name of the construction company. Words in black would be illuminated from behind by powerful bulbs. The words were not yet written though, so here I was.

There was no chain-link fence, either, so I walked straight up to the thing unhindered, I clambered on to the base, scraping my knees, and felt the metal beneath my hands. It seemed still warm from the sun that had set over three hours ago. Lines of bolts curved beneath my palm, each one as big as an eyeball. They felt like goosebumps. Clare's skin would rise like that when I brushed my hands along her sides. I looked up to see how the crane bent away into the sky. From this angle the moon was thin and flat, like the fluorescent lamps they used in the corridors at my middle school. I lowered my gaze, slightly dazzled, and reached out to touch the stem of the crane. My hands found rungs, a black ladder. I held on with both hands for a second, before the smoke from the Lucky Strike stub hurt my eyes. I took the butt and flicked it back onto the gravel path where it exploded into sparks. 'Goodbye, Earth,' I almost said, 'We've had some times.' I began to climb at fourteen minutes after midnight.

Ten minutes later I was at the top and the moon was almost within arm's reach. I pulled myself onto the small round platform and sat down heavily, leaning against the controller's box and letting my arms fall to my sides while I caught my breath. After a while I took the box of Lucky Strikes from my jacket pocket but it was empty. These things wouldn't burn on the surface of the moon anyway, I thought. I threw them off the side of the platform with a flick, but couldn't hear the impact 60 metres below. I stood up and inhaled deeply, drawing in warm summer air that was as yet unscented, having not quite fallen to the height of the trees. I lowered myself gently onto the long arm of the crane and crawled along it for a couple of metres. The metal was cooler up here. When I reached the moon, I stopped and rose unsteadily to my feet, not looking down for a second. The rectangle moon was directly beneath my feet. I could have been standing on its frame. There was a fierce heat coming from the moon.

I could feel it on my ankles and through the rubber soles of my trainers. I spread my arms for balance, and allowed myself to look out into the night. I could see the lights of a city, the swells of the hills. I even thought that I could see, on the edge of the western horizon, the faint glow of the sun as it disappeared beneath the Earth. The Earth. I looked down to see the ground, but I couldn't quite make it out through the glare of the rectangle moon. No Earth. It made sense to me then. I spread my arms as wide as I could and turned to face the east, letting the wind fill me like a sail.

13____tim harding

It's not exactly stalking. Not stalking. Enthusiastic following, maybe. But definitely not stalking. He's not exactly going out of his way just to see her. The train he used to catch was only faster by twenty-three minutes and anyway this way he gets to drink his coffee slowly instead of sploshing it all over his silk ties. Rushing around like an idiot every morning is not good for his health and it certainly isn't good for his expensive tie collection. She would be good for him. She would be magnificent every morning. He sees her wrapped in white silk sheets, her bronze skin glowing in the morning sun sneaking through the blinds, sneaking in to see her legs curl around him. He can feel her soft lips on his neck waking him gently. She pulls the sheets from him and pulls him into the bathroom, pushing him up against the ice cold tiles, letting steam and water rise and fall between them as she eases him in and out of her.

He waits for his train, polystyrene coffee cup in one hand, leather briefcase in the other. He glances up and down the platform, anticipating the woollen coat and stiletto heels. He looks at his watch and taps his shoe against the concrete nervously, as the train arrives before the stilettos.

He hesitates before he steps onto the train. He wonders where she is. She's never once been late. Not once in two months and thirteen days. He reluctantly gets on, takes a seat near the door just in case she gets there as the train pulls away and he can hold the door and help her on board. But the whistle blows and the door clicks shut and there is no woollen coat, no stiletto shoes.

And then he sees her long finger-nails tracing shadows on her lover's neck, her shining hair tossed to one side as her legs curl around him and she pushes herself into him, moaning gently as he slides in and out of her, his strong hands gripping the small of her back. He can see her lover smashing the ringing alarm clock against the wall, rolling her onto her back as he kisses her lips, her neck, her breasts, her stomach, her thighs.

He takes the last sip of coffee from his cup, its bitter taste clinging to the back of his throat, and crushes the polystyrene against the table with his fist. He wants to get off the train and storm over to her apartment. He wants to break down the door and tear the man from her, smash him against the wall, wrap her in silk sheets and take her home with him. He wants to smooth her hair and kiss her head and make her some sweet tea. He wants to stop dreaming about her. Two months and thirteen days and he doesn't even know her name. She probably hasn't even noticed him. Two months and thirteen days wasted on a woman who probably wouldn't look at him twice anyway.

Today is the day. Definitely. She combs her hair in the mirror. She sees him walking up behind her in the reflection, pushing her shining hair over her shoulder, tickling her neck with his soft lips. She can feel his strong grip around her shoulders. Two months and fourteen days and not a word. She thinks he's shy. She has decided he hasn't even noticed her. She wants to speak to him. She wants to go for a drink, order a bottle of white wine. She wants to feel his large hand sliding up her smooth leg. She wants to pull him into her bedroom, push him onto her bed. She can feel his fingers stroking her hair as she kisses his neck, his chest, his stomach, she can feel his fingers tracing patterns in her skin as she unzips his trousers with her teeth.

She is determined to speak to him today. She is determined to look gorgeous and get him to notice her. She rises from her dresser. She takes the satin dress from its hanger. She can feel the silk caressing her hips. She can feel his hands on her. Her hand trembles as she applies gloss to her lips. She doesn't have time for a cup of coffee to steady her nerves and she doesn't want to risk soaking her satin dress. She smiles at her reflection in the mirror.

She takes her watch from the dresser and looks at it as she fastens it around her slender wrist. She is late. She slips on her stiletto shoes and woollen coat. She rushes down the stairs and out into the street, slamming the doors shut. She hurries around the corner and down the steps into the station. The train is always on time. She hopes she hasn't missed it. Her heels click on the metal steps down to the platform. It is empty. The train has gone. He has gone. Two months and fourteen days and today was going to be the day. She was sure of it. Her heels echo on the concrete as she walks over to a bench. She slumps on the cold metal and stares out onto the empty tracks. She wants to wait in the station all day for him until he comes back. She doesn't want to feel like a stalker. She wonders if it would count as stalking. She wonders if maybe it would just be enthusiastic following. Two months and fourteen days and she doesn't even know his name. He probably hasn't even noticed her. Two months and fourteen days wasted on a man who probably wouldn't look at her twice anyway.

It's the colours of the clothes which most surprise you. Memory has greyed those Barbie-doll-pink shorts, that egg-yolk yellow jacket; the roll-neck pea-green jumper worn with turquoise, half-mast cords.

Long-forgotten is the emerald of that velvet bridesmaid's dress, or the coral of the one the year before, the day your father collared you in the vestry of the church, hissing how from this day on he would expect you to call his new wife 'Mum'.

So there you all now are in those happy family slides. In this one you are gazing out across the windy cliff-tops high above the Whitby coast in some party-frock festooned with scarlet poppies large as dinner-plates. And here again – please say it wasn't you – outside the little Bistro in the market-place at Carcassonne. Aged, what, about thirteen, sipping your bulb-bottled Orangina through your chewed-up paper straw; there in the unforgiving glare of rucksack-ed, denim-ed tourists in your cheap, red-plastic flip-flops and that just darling strapless sundress dancing with swirling galaxies of phosphorescent lime.

A lifetime's cardboard-framed transparencies; lift them out of their dark filing-cases, watch the colours spring to life – vivid greens and sunshine yellows, big skies of travel-brochure azure and seas of stunning peacock blue. Place them before your eyes, those deep pinks and reds and oranges. Closer. Hold them high against the sunlight; note the clouds on the horizon, the sallow tinge behind your apple-cheeks, the dazzling whiteness of those overexposed smiles. See, in these patches where the colours pale, as it is with clear lenses, just how easy it becomes to look straight through.

_BLUE RASPBERRY

You walk out of the gate, the black iron gate, pieces of rust in the corners, rough against your fingers. You close it behind you, fasten the latch. You walk across your concrete, looking down at your shoes; blue with a t-bar, showing your bare, brown skin through the little windows. Your legs are bare too, your shorts looking newly washed white against your coffee skin. You step onto the gravel of the alley, the stones crunching under your feet, kicking up dust like the pieces at the bottom of your cereal packet. The air smells hot, close around your mouth and nose, like a pillow suffocating you and your throat scratches with the beginnings of hay fever.

The fence to the right is falling down. You go and push it, remembering how the old lady who lives there shouted at you before for throwing your ball over. It's rough, old, like the old lady, splinters of decaying wood searching out your skin. It creaks as you push it, like her voice, high-pitched and whining, telling you to keep away. You don't want her to catch you. They say she's a witch. It was fun before with your friends, laughing at her, then running away. It's not the same on your own.

You stop when you come to the telegraph pole and stand there staring at it, as if staring out an enemy. The fear in your stomach becomes something else, something hard. You bend down and pick up a stone, feel its warm smoothness in your damp hand, the sharp edge digging in your skin, smooth, but at the same time sharp. You throw it hard at the solid wooden pole and it bounces off, becoming lost amongst the other stones all the same. You touch the pole, put your hand where the stone struck it, feel the wood, smooth, not like the old fence, and remember when you were partners, two days ago, or maybe three. You cannot decide if that makes it your friend or your enemy. They tied one end of the rope to the pole and made you hold the other one, made you turn and turn, while they skipped on and on: salt, mustard, vinegar, pepper... You stood still and silent like the telephone pole, only your hand moving, your arm growing heavy and something hard, like a stone growing inside your stomach. Then you dropped the rope, the wooden handle thudding against the concrete; her concrete, not yours. They tripped and shouted at you, the rope tangled round their ankles like a snake. But you just walked on, back to your house where you coughed up the hardness in your stomach.

Now you walk on, up to the old sycamore tree, so tall it hurts your neck to look up at the top. You place your hand on the rough bark, tracing the groves shaped over time. You go behind the tree into the secret place. It smells damp, earthy, like the sweet smell of fruit just going bad. You sit down amongst the newly fallen leaves, the older, rotting leaves hidden beneath. Mixed with them are discarded ice-pole wrappers. You pick one up, see the trace of blue raspberry in the bottom. You remember her sitting there eating it, sucking it, the colour the same as her eyes. She offered the blue pole to you and you closed your hands around it, feeling the cold seep into them. You put it to your lips, tasting the icy sweet-sharpness, your lips becoming numb. Then you smiled at her with your frozen lips, that time in the secret camp, that time you were friends.

Now you crush the plastic in your hand, let it fall amongst the rotting leaves.

And you think how raspberries are not blue.

Abs is sitting on the worktop holding a bottle of kitchen bleach spray. She's telling me about this guy her boss used to know.

Pft. 'Got one. Look at it squirm.' (The spray's for the ants that are invading our kitchen this summer.) *Pft.* 'They're all coming out, the stupid bastards. If you bang the worktop they think it's food.' *Bang, bang* with her fist on the worktop. *Pft.* 'Look at them!'

'You were saying?' I ask. I'm standing on the other side of the room, leaning on the sink with my white shirt un-tucked.

'Yeah, so Andy knows this guy who's just broken a world record.'

'Yeah?'

'Yeah. Guess what the world record is.'

I hold my fingertips to my chin. 'Table-tennis-table-hopping?'

Pft. 'Hah. No. Shark-baiting. This guy's got a world record for pissing off Great Whites.'

'Is that possible?'

'Must be.' She nods enthusiastically. *Pft.* 'He did it in the Pacific, I think. Just went out on a boat to see how many he could rile up.'

'The nutcase.'

'I *know*.'

The day before last we had an argument. A stupid one about money, as per. If we ever argue then it's about money. Abs was working things out for when we move in August and I wanted to wait. I wanted to see how things were when we got there, rather than nailing down every penny.

We were in bed. I was propped up against pillows with a tea in hand and she was on her front, scrawling in her red-spotted notebook. Numbers everywhere, in no logical order.

'Can't we just leave it for now?' I said.

'Of course we can't fucking leave it! If we leave it we'll fritter everything away in July and have nothing left to kit the new place out with.'

'Kit the new place out?'

She shrugged. 'Sofa? Fridge? Washing machine? *God*, you can be an idiot when you want to.'

I ran the tip of my forefinger around the rim of my tea mug.

'Just help me out, will you?' she said.

'Okay, well my wage packet should be...'

Argument over. Winner declared.

Right now the ants are losing. I look over Abs' left shoulder and there are five or six sprawled out in patches of acrid smelling bleach. One's still struggling for air, its little legs waving and spinning in front of it, and then it dies. They're all crumpled in little balls.

'Funny how even ants revert to the foetal position when they die,' I say into Abs' ear.

'Yeah,' she says back.

I make a fake stomach pain noise and stagger back towards the sink. Abs follows, laughing, poking me in the ribs. She pokes me right through the flat and into the bedroom and we're both laughing, and the poking carries on right to the bed. She spins me, grabs my right forearm with her left hand and draws her right hand up into the air to grab my left. Fuck, she still has the fucking bleach, and I can see it coming all the way down through the air as she slips, her fingers jerk, and there's a piercing *pft* and then just pain.

I scream. Then Abs screams. I'm saying, 'Get some fucking water, fuck!' and Abs runs out of the room and all's quiet for a second. Then pain again, right through my eyeballs and round the top of my cheeks, into my sinuses, up through my scalp and down the back of my neck. I try to open my eyes and oh, oh, God, it's so much worse. Stabs of forked lightening directly into the synapses.

Abs is back with a tub of warm water and a flannel, and the phone clamped between her teeth. She dips the flannel in the water and then pushes me back on the bed, mounts me and dabs at my eyes. The water just surrounds the pain. Accentuates it. With her now free hand she pulls the phone from between her teeth and she's dialling three numbers with the same tone of beep and then she's putting the phone to her face.

I can barely see through the red, puffed-up flesh but I stop struggling now. I stop clawing at my face and Abs stops too. She relaxes on top of me but still dabs at my eyes and I slump, slump into the pillows with my eyes clamped shut and feel the burn, the sizzle, and I'm picturing those five or six ants all curled up in the foetal position, little legs protruding in panic into the air, and I'm feeling the burning sensation consume my head.

The phone's at my ear now.

'Hello? Hello?'

'I'm fine,' I say. 'It just stings a bit.

'Why does he have a swastika on his chest?' I pointed to the picture of the giant Buddha and tilted the page so Brian could see.

Brian had been asleep but looked now at where I was pointing. 'It's Sanskrit; in Hindu and Buddhist religions it means well-being.' I hadn't meant to wake him but I'd been engrossed in my tour guide and hadn't noticed him and Holly nod off.

'Ah, ok,' I said and let him get back to sleep, though I didn't know how he could. The hill was slanted almost vertically and the bus was so heavy I worried that it would topple and send us falling like a brick downstairs. *If the driver stalls then we're done for.*

I wasn't so nervous that I wouldn't look out the window. Off road in-between trees and sand hills were villages that stood like lilies on a pond. I saw a tiny lady of about forty hanging up some washing. She ignored the passing coach just as animals at a zoo might ignore gawping onlookers.

Holly tapped me on the shoulder. 'Brian's grandparents live in a village like that.' She was keen for me to understand that Hong Kong wasn't just forty-storey flats with laundry hanging on poles from the windows.

'They seem peaceful,' I said.

'I think we're almost there,' said Holly, trying to get a look at what was beyond the immediate view of the window. She nudged Brian, whose head had hit the back of his seat again.

I realised once the bus stopped that this whole trip was for me. Brian and Holly had already seen it and were more excited about the meat on sticks being sold at the stalls than the giant Buddha saying a silent 'how' from the mountain-top. 'Shall I meet you in Starbucks?' I asked. They were giggling and poking each other as they ran off.

I'd had to stay close to Brian and Holly all week. Now, as I began to climb the stairs towards the Tian Tan Buddha, I felt as if I'd been let loose like a helium balloon reaching for the sky.

Branches obscured the Buddha from where I was standing at the bottom. Once I'd climbed twenty or so stairs I could just make out his outline but details such as the swastika were not yet visible. I added some flight to my step.

He seemed relaxed sitting there. If I were that big I would worry about imposing on other people's space but he seemed confident that the spot on top of the mountain was meant for him. The coloured dots of people were moving silently up and down the stairs. Nobody seemed to want to overtake anyone else. The Buddha's right arm was raised but he seemed to be looking over their heads. The left hand's fingers were slightly curled as if he were saying *come hither then.*

At the bottom, branches obscured him. Halfway up his outline was visible. After that the closer I got the less I could see of him. He was too big for my field of vision. At no point could I see the swastika.

I reached the top and all I could see of him was rounded blank bronze jutting out at me. His bottom obscured the top from view. I walked the top circle, around and around, but from here it just seemed like a bronze wall.

Lady statues bent on one knee were holding out candles and lotus flowers for him. They could see him then. The corners of their mouths seemed to be twitching upwards as if beneath the unchanging expressions they were secretly smug. I jumped so they might see me but their heads were held up and they were too tall.

I wondered how high up I was. I couldn't make out the faces of the people on the Earth but the sun setting over us didn't seem any closer. I wondered why we all came here. I hadn't found anything much to see.

It was dark when we got on the coach and the Tan Tian Buddha was lit up from the bottom on his spot on the mountain. He stared straight ahead and couldn't see our coach as it pulled away

The child lies on the stone veranda gazing at the sapphire-blue world that is boundless. Cauliflower clouds constantly re-shape themselves as they drift across – one turns into a dragon with puffs of smoke curling from its mouth. The child's skin feels sticky. She rolls over and peeps through a hole in the wall at the other world that is holding its breath under the fierce sunlight.

A tall wicker hat emerges from the jungle darkness and bobs through the long grass. Beneath the hat is a seller of wild bananas. Bunches of plump yellow fingers sway from a pole stretched across his shoulders as he trots through the clearing.

The child, recalling the sweet taste of the fruit, runs from the house and leaps across the ditches that protect it from the monsoon rains. Her bare feet alight on the burning-hot road as she almost collides with the man.

His mouth dominates his face, pushing the sallow skin into creases, narrowing the eyes. The broken teeth and gold fillings leer at the child.

'Missy like bananas – yes?'

The child thinks of a smiling dragon and is unsure about the sweetness of *his* bananas. She runs home.

That evening after the sun has fallen quickly from the sky the child is taken on a bus. People cram onto it; this is a special occasion. She shares in the excitement of their high-pitched, singsong voices. They arrive in the city where it seems as if a million people are surging towards a clangorous dragon-procession.

Gold and red spirals on the dragon's body swirl to the beat of drums; flames leap from its mouth as the gongs resound. Fire torches flicker in the frenzied dance. Silks and cottons with their various perfumes brush against her face.

'Keep hold of my hand!' calls her mother.

But in the confusion of elbows and legs the child is swallowed into the crowd.

She searches frantically amongst the medley of colours and faces until they become a watery blur. The procession has reached the shoreline and the child believes that she has become one of the dragon's shining scales that are spreading across the sand as it plunges into the sea. The spell is broken by an explosion of colour in the sky. The dragon emerges from the water, but it has a different guise.

The child wanders across the Padang where merchants squat next to their wares spread on mats. Smells of burning joss-sticks, spices, dried fish, curries, kerosene and roasted peanuts mingle together, providing a strange comfort. But it is not the comfort she's seeking. As she passes an array of tropical fruits a familiar face appears before her. But it is not the face she seeks. This one is exposing ugly gold-teeth.

A hand beckons and a banana is thrust towards her. 'Missy like – Yes?'

The child has learnt to shout '*Ta, pigee-la, pigee-la!*' ('No, go away, go away!')

As she staggers backwards arms envelop her. Her face presses against flesh with the scent of the one that she was seeking. The dragon vanishes like a puff of cloud.

_THE APERITIF

Although you do not know your aunt's neighbours well, you feel that Monsieur L's recent successful brain operation requires some kind of gesture from you. He has already resumed work on his exterior garden wall, a fortress-like construction around half a metre thick. You have brought him a box of fudge, from England.

But your gift has got you into trouble – it has resulted in an invitation for an aperitif that evening, when you would rather be next door, clearing Aunt C's house, looking through photographs and marvelling at how young and beautiful she was once, hair down her back, or up in a French pleat, in a bikini, Biarritz '62 or Bretagne '69. How you'd like to keep the house as a museum to her memory, with its collection of camembert boxes on the dining room wall, the felt clown dangling from a light fitting, candle-sticks, Moulinex graters, mocha machines, herbal remedies, obsolete radio alarm clocks, audio typewriting equipment and boxes of walnuts she gathered two years ago, preserved intact.

This year has yielded another bumper crop. You can feel them through your trainers like pebbles on a beach. You didn't know this was how walnuts arrived on earth. You are filled with wonder at the soft caul which envelops each one, sticky like damson jam or a blood clot, staining your hands like engine oil. And the shells so tender and wrinkly, like a baby's head.

The two boys are sitting at table with mugs of soup when you arrive. You sit next to little Guillaume, who smiles charmingly as he tries to reach inside his pyjama trousers. His mother places his hands on the table, like the town sheriff. His father puts a plate of crêpes on the table; this will be their reward for drinking their soup.

But there is trouble lifting up silently around you like a yellow familiar mist. Guillaume is more interested in crêpes than in his soup. He is employing several clumsy techniques for not drinking the greenish liquid. 'It is too hot,' he says, looking at you as if to corroborate this, and you smile, knowing this is a game like the ones you would have played. Even the attempt at crying is something you recognise. As the youngest in your family you employed this technique often enough yourself. What you haven't noticed is that his father's voice, which began almost pleasantly, now has a steely menace to it, and has become a growl. Suddenly he seizes the boy by the ear and removes him to the kitchen. You are surprised at this. Guillaume's lack of interest in soup didn't seem a major transgression, nor did his whimpering. But the sound of him being beaten through the kitchen wall is real, though you remain seated, staring into middle distance. The older boy looks at you with a sad, knowing smile, and attempts to make strangely adult small talk. *This has happened before, must happen often*, you think.

25___frances knight

What a coward I am, you say to yourself. But you hardly know these people and if you say something they will – what? Tell you that they'll do as they please in their own home, remind you that you have no children? But should you make it so easy for them, feigning interest in the older boy's flute lessons, their walnut trees, each a different species, their apples which they have pressed into juice, delicious, you say. In the dark, you picture your aunt's apples fermenting on the lawn next door. You'd like to be back there now.

You discuss your Aunt's house, omitting almost every detail that is important to you, concentrating on the drainage and the wasp colony in the roof. Mr L shows you his scar which is concealed behind his ear. The hair has grown back nicely, you nod. After some time, Guillaume is allowed back. You watch his face closely – it seems to have a terrible little smile burning inside. He eats a crêpe, and afterwards shows you a butterfly costume made last year at a children's art workshop. It is made from a huge expanse of white paper, skilfully folded and draped into huge wings, more like those of an angel than a butterfly. You are amazed that, given its fragility, this costume has survived so long. Guillaume has doe eyes, you think, something sweetly girlish. This is when you realise that his father does not like him, and you feel it like a slap on the side of your own head.

Finally you leave, cross through to the adjoining garden. In the stillness you hear a TGV shudder past, gulping the distance between here and Paris, as surely as Paris will one day swallow up this small town. You imagine a future Guillaume, whose mother will be pale and stiff as a doll when he brings home his boyfriend who is a lorry driver. His father will refuse to come into the house, he will be at the far end of the garden mixing concrete, or chopping off the branch of a walnut tree.

'No!'

'It's not your wall.'

'No.' He taps off some ash, it floats on the lumpy puddle. Chilli-sauce, what looks like frogspawn, and scraps of doner meat. It's lit up, pinkish, by the take-out place's electric sign.

'Wow. Euck. That wasn't you, was it?'

'Me?' He sucks on his cigarette and looks up, blowing smoke at the black sky, watching his puffs drift then disappear. 'Check out the other side.'

She pushes up against the cold brick and looks behind him. Dirt, dead plants, bits of green glass... and a half-buried condom. Used. She reaches into the pouch on her dress – a tiny digital camera comes out. She lines up the lens, and a silver-white flash makes his eyes go funny.

'What you doing? Why are you dressed like a kangaroo?' Without thinking it through, he pats the brick next to his other leg.

She gets up next to him, no problem. 'You hungry?'

'Errrr... Kind of.'

She skips off, and he figures that she'll never come back. From where he sits on top of the wall he can see someone having what looks like a one-sided fight. More of a beating. A tall, skinny boy is putting the boot in – a balled-up someone screams from down on the pavement. Groups of people hang around to chuck chips or snap pictures. The beating ends when the balled-up someone rolls into the road and gets hit by a passing Land Rover.

Then she comes back. 'Lettuce?'

'Is that all you got?'

'Uh-huh.'

'Go on then.'

They sit there, legs dangling, picking shredded lettuce out of a polystyrene box. He tells her about the accident. She tells him to tell her exactly what happened, then takes a picture of him smoking. The boy who's been beaten up and run-over isn't dead. They can see him queuing up inside the take-out place.

When his bus comes, he doesn't get on. It's packed and looks like trouble. Five minutes it takes to get away from the stop – a group of men go ballistic, spitting at the driver, demanding to be let on for child's rate.

Her hands are shaking. He says come on, take my jacket, but she makes it clear that she wants to be cold, for now. 'Blow your smoke in my face.' She closes her eyes, and he does as he is told.

Another photo – their cheeks touching, their faces serious. They talk about how weird everything is. They find out that they both like sugar and lemon AND treacle on their pancakes – they both prefer Weller's solo stuff.

When he says he has work tomorrow, she cries into her fists. He stabs out his cigarette on the brick, and carries on stabbing it out. She tells him to kiss her tears. He says he'll do anything, just anything. Name it.

'Throw away your cigarettes. In a bin – not in with the plants.'

Done.

She puts her blue hands into the pouch. 'Take me home.'

He follows her up the stairs. They carry their shoes in their hands.

'Don't worry about making a noise,' she says, 'no one else is in. This is my room.'

The TV has been left on. Just a blue screen, but enough light to see by. He checks out the walls – all painted a plain light blue. The ceiling's the same.

'Where's your stuff?'

She's plugging the digital camera into a PC. 'I've got rid of most of it. It's better having the space.'

As the photos download, she takes off her dress, folds it up and stuffs it under her single bed. Her underwear goes the same way.

'How old are you?' he says.

She stares at the computer screen. There they are – both looking young and serious. 'You've got to see this.' She double-clicks, double-clicks. A slideshow begins – one photo dissolves into another, every five or so seconds.

He sees a fat man. Pencil moustache. Wearing a lime-green hard hat. The hat is tipped down so that it's close to his eyes...

A traffic warden. Next to a BMW with a ticket stuck to its windscreen. A McDonalds sign at the top of the photo...

A girl, say twenty. Only wearing black knickers. Foam, fluffy grey-silver foam from her waist to her neck. Blowing a kiss...

A PLEASE PUT YOUR GUM IN THE BIN sign dotted with gum. Nike trainers and stiletto heels on the pavement. A pair of stonewashed jeans, a pair of pasty legs...

'Who are they?'

She's lifting the duvet at the foot of the bed. She crawls in. He watches the lumps budge up towards the pillows. 'I don't know,' she says, shouting from beneath the covers. 'They're people and things I've seen. I bet you've never watched *The Wizard of Oz*.'

'I have. I have. Ages ago.'

'Press play on the TV.'

He takes off his clothes, and, because she asks him to, stuffs them under the bed. He presses play and squeezes in beside her. 'The computer. Should I turn it off?'

'No,' she says, holding him down. 'I like to let it run all night.' The screen carries on showing different people, different places.

They watch the whole of *The Wizard of Oz*. Then they watch the bonus disc.

'I'll go out early,' he says, 'and get what we need for pancakes.'

A twenty-second snatch of music, from the film, plays on a permanent loop. A milk float, from outside, hums through the silence. She wriggles backwards, still closer to him. He guesses that, like him, she wants to sleep.

I used to love pretending to sleep on you. I remember feeling the sudden shift of your old shirt on your skin as you coughed, or the buzz of your chest when you laughed at the telly. Occasionally, you'd gently rake your fingers through my hair up to the elastic band that held it back, and sometimes you moved me slightly if my head slid onto the hard, uncomfortable part of your collar bone. Sometimes I laid my head on the puppy rolls of your stomach, my elbow slotted into the triangle of your crotch, my thumb in gentle rhythm over your waist, back and forth, slowing to a stop. I know you always hated your little bulges, but I loved them. The way your belly hung over your jeans slightly, the way a muffin is over its paper cup. It was cute.

One night last week it took you longer than usual to notice that I was 'sleeping' and when you did, you shunted me off and 'woke me up.'

'Sleepy?' you asked.

'No,' I said. 'Not at all.' I was amazed that you didn't understand.

Last night, I dozed on the hard arm of the sofa. I dropped off through the tail end of the news as our plates sat abandoned near our feet, stained red-brown from the spaghetti, all through *Friends*. Clever quips and canned laughter. I hated it but I knew you'd watch it so I didn't bother opening my eyes. As I heard the credits roll, I felt the square chunk of sofa cushion rock underneath me as you got up to stack our plates. I yawned and stretched but didn't open my eyes. 'I'll do that,' I said. 'Just gimme five minutes.' My feet were freezing.

'You cooked.'

'Yeah, but I have to get my socks anyway.'

'What does it matter? I'm up already.' I felt a little raft of cold air as you walked off to the kitchen, and I heard you dump the plates on the side. You wouldn't wash them.

That was the longest conversation we'd had so far that evening. The half hour after we both got in from work, and then the whole time I was cooking, we hadn't exchanged more words than that. It used to be that if I was cooking and you were watching telly, I'd take you a bit of raw red pepper, tell you to shut your eyes in that cheesy Romantic Comedy way, and then put it on your tongue like you were a hungry baby bird. I didn't do that last night. You might just eat it without shutting your eyes, like you did last time, or worse, wave me away, irritated.

I stretched again, and then got up and padded into the bedroom to get my socks. You'd picked the lilac for the room. Carpet, curtains, and duvet. I used to love the colour lilac. The window was open, and I shut it with a hollow plastic thud. Once, I picked you up and threw you on that bed. What happened then had surprised both of us and afterwards, we actually smoked in there. That's the only time I remember us even thinking about doing that. Probably the last.

I was just shutting the door to the bedroom, and I noticed the faint smell of smoke in the hallway so I knew you'd lit a cigarette. I heard your voice, from the sitting room, saying, 'shut the door.'

I *always* do. I used to leave it open by accident sometimes, when we first moved in, but it was a habit you hated so much I made a point of never, ever doing it. Now it's become so ingrained, I haven't forgotten for about a year. Probably more.

'Of course,' I said, standing in the doorway of the sitting room, folded arms, leaning on the frame. 'Hey, do you remember that time we smoked in there?'

'Yeah.' Your eyes were fixed on the telly. You flicked the buttons, and stopped on another channel, another episode of *Friends*. A late one, after Chandler and Monica married, when it got boring. Just about when I stopped watching it.

'I picked you up and threw you on the bed...' I went over to the sofa, perched on the arm, and stroked your hair.

'I remember.' You held my hand in yours so it couldn't move anymore. The programme broke for adverts but you didn't take your eyes off the telly. 'Listen, are you going to do those dishes or not? Cos if not, I'll do them now, while the adverts are on.'

The advert was for car insurance: loud and cheap, with a bright green dancing phone. I took my hand off your head, got up, went into the kitchen and started to fill up the bowl. The plates were white with a thick blue band round the outside, dotted with dark purple olives. I didn't rinse the bubbles off the plates, like you always used to tell me to do.

When I'd finished the pots and the lot was dripping dry on the draining board, I set up two mugs for tea and filled the kettle. I knew that I just had time to put two teabags in the mugs and two dashes of milk, and scrub the tomato scum line from the washing up bowl while the water came to the boil.

Just as the kettle started shaking and steaming, I went to throw the washing up sponge away and saw that the bin was on the brink of over-flowing, so I left the tea, tied up the bag and started to slowly slide it out of the bin that came up with it. I let the bin drop on the lino with a dull thud. I knotted the old bag and leaned it against the door, and then flapped out a fresh bin bag before putting it back in the cupboard. I then took the full bag, heavy and slightly greasy, slid on a pair of old pink slippers that I always left by the door, and started down the fire escape.

It had been raining all day, and everything I could see was blackened with night and damp, apart from the ruby necklaces of car brake lights snaking the roads. I liked the fact we lived on the third floor. It was high enough but not too high.

The fire escape, metal with black paint flaking off, was slippery, so I held the cold iron rail, feeling how it swayed a little in the wind that came in little gusts. At the bottom of the stairs I stepped onto the shiny concrete that seemed to flash orange from the streetlights on the main road. I could hear the traffic over the high wall, a soft, grey, whooshing sound. I opened up the lid and hoisted the bag into one the wheelies, feeling something drip down my leg. Probably water. I slammed the lid and left my hand on it, squashing some fat cold raindrops that trembled in the wind like tiny, clear jellies.

I stood there for a minute, watching the rain, thinking how it looked like lots of little needles floating toward me. Most were white, and some were shining orange in the light. I tipped my head right back, my mouth wide open in the blackness. The air and rain tasted like dirt. I felt the cold wet from the ground seep through the worn fur of my slippers and I imagined someone looking back at me from the sky, like a dark overhead shot in a film.

In the kitchen, I made up the two mugs of tea, and slipped an ashtray and half a bar of Dairy Milk under my arm to take back into the lounge with me. 'Thanks,' you said, sitting up as I put the tea next to the sofa leg nearest your head.

'Shall I roll a joint?'

'Alright.' You slid the rolling box over the carpet to me. Silver, lined with felt. I think your sister's cutlery set came in it. I sat cross-legged on the floor and rolled on a copy of *Take-a-Break* on the coffee table. I only got it sometimes for the puzzles. There was a story in it about a woman who married a murderer. I got bored of telly pretty quickly. Still *Friends*. I wanted to ask you to change the channel. 'Are you happy?' I asked, when I sat back and lit the joint.

'Happy?' you repeated. I knew your real answer then. Happiness doesn't question itself.

'Yeah,' I said. 'You know... contented.'

'Yeah.' And then you said, 'Are you?'

I knew that your question was an afterthought and blew grey smoke out of my nostrils. 'Yeah,' I lied.

In bed. I was a bit stoned, but not very much. We didn't smoke like we used to – we always seemed to have work the next day. 'Are you sure you're happy?' I asked.

'Huh?'

'Earlier. I asked you if you were happy. You said 'Yeah'. But are you... you know, *sure*?' I folded my arm under my head so I could lie on it. I could see the white fleshy bit of my upper arm out the corner of my eye.

'Yeah. Why?'

Things were different at night. At night, I could talk. Or try, at least. I took a deep breath. 'Well, we don't talk like we used to.' I thought you might get angry, but you didn't.

'We don't really need to. All that 'getting to know each other' stuff stops after a while.' I could tell that your eyes were closed and you really wanted to sleep.

'But I don't know everything about you. And you don't know everything about me.' My words sounded as pathetic as wet petals but you didn't seem to notice.

'That's not really what I meant... it's just something that happens in relationships. Nothing to worry about.'

'I wasn't worried.' I rolled over, my back to you, and listened to my breath in the dark as if I was afraid of it.

I was up early this morning. About six. I slipped out of bed quickly, without looking at your sleeping face, pulled on a jumper and padded into the kitchen. The flat was cold, but smelled like central heating – damp and musty. The mute green carpet and the dusty dried flowers on the table in the hall seemed two-dimensional in their flat blandness. I hated seeing the same objects every day. The thought of seeing those same pink-brown dried flowers every day forever made me feel weary, like I was hearing my alarm but was already awake.

I filled the kettle and set up two mugs for tea. As it boiled, I put away last night's plates and the two saucepans, which were now dry. Despite the cold, I opened the door that led to the fire escape, put on my old slippers, and stepped out, mouth open in the sharp air. Lots of little blobs of cloud filled the sky, making it look like a blue and white leopard's skin. Some bits, especially where the sun was rising, were tinged pink, and around the bottom, next to the grey houses and shops in the town, there was a strip that was almost lilac.

I wanted you to see it with me. I really did. I wanted to go and peel you out of bed, cup my hands over your eyes, lead you to the door by your hand, and make you stand on the fire escape, where I would whip my hand away and I would see you gasp at the speckled sky. I wanted to talk with you about how it would look from another angle, and how it is that the air can have colour, and then for a long time perhaps I could just hold you in the cold, and we'd look at it until the clouds had melted away into something else, and the day had woken up.

But I didn't do anything. I stood there in the morning light alone. I stood there and looked and looked and looked at those clouds. I knew that these sights did not last forever and I wanted to take it in, take it all in while I could, while it was here, since I was here too. Before it was gone.

I wanted to scream into the sky.

I wanted to make sure that I never forgot it.

'What're you doing out there?' Your voice in the kitchen. 'It's fucking cold.'

I didn't say anything, but turned away from the view and came back in. Our kitchen seemed gloomy after standing under the brightness of the sky. You were standing barefoot, shivering on the lino, your arms crossed in your baggy fleece top, your hands hidden in your armpits. 'You've been out there ages.' You made it sound like an accusation and as I shut the door, I suddenly felt very self-conscious, as if I'd been caught rifling through your pockets for receipts.

'Not really. Not too long.' I paused. 'I don't think.'

You clicked the kettle to boil the water again. 'Half an hour you've been out there.'

I looked at the time on the microwave. 6.24. 'You were asleep half an hour ago.'

'No, I wasn't.'

I caught the look in your eyes as the kettle started shuddering again and you turned away. And I knew that I should have guessed.

'I was just dozing,' you said.

He wears a worn green T-shirt printed with the words: *Cuba, Libya, Germany.* I know he thinks it makes him look political, edgy even. With ill-fitting worn jeans, a scarf (even though it must be 25 degrees outside), a shadow of beard and tousled hair, he plays the impoverished artist well; a crafted illusion which belies the fact he is already very successful and owns a converted sail loft apartment on the seafront. To Matt, everything is secondary to the making of the image.

I've already finished my second latté. I wave him over and watch as he snakes his way through the tables, pursing his lips into the delicious apologetic pout that always pushes my buttons. I pull at the front of his T-shirt, pretending to read the slogan. 'You're as late as ever. And still lying to yourself, I see, you sad bastard.' Matt smiles. When he looks at you, it's an intense, searching look, which makes you feel completely absorbed by him. It has power; it consumes.

'Yeah, sorry. But you know... work 'n' all. Lost track. Look, babe, I know I said we'd eat out, but I'm in the middle of something right now and have to get back to the studio. You've just gotta come back with me. I really need you.'

I want to punish him for his negligence, his habitual lateness, the fact that I'm always too eager to please him, but his energy and enthusiasm catch me by surprise and I'm flattered into submission. I haven't seen him for weeks and when I have managed to get him on the phone, he's been moody and argumentative. It's good to see him so animated.

The apartment and studio are one and the same. Although it was an expensive conversion some four years previously, the minimalist interior soon became cluttered with the trappings of an artist's lifestyle. The stripped pine floors are stained in inks and the heady scent of oil-based paint has gradually permeated all the soft furnishings. I find it an intoxicating mix, and have given up trying to tidy away even the smallest space for 'us'. Matt is into his space. Matt says he has to live and breathe his art before, during and after its creation. Matt's space is his inspiration and his canvas.

His unmade bed sits central in the room with unfinished works still dripping colour, jostling for space with a range of ornately-framed mirrors suspended on wire hooks from the exposed timbers above. I feel uncomfortable watching prismatic images of my naked self flashing into view at crazy angles. I complain to Matt, but he loves it of course; his eyes never leave the spectacle. Now, I just keep mine shut.

Today Matt is wired. There's an urgency, a hunger about him and he doesn't recognise my need for breath as he rushes me along the narrow streets towards the studio. The familiar rush of linseed and turpentine hits me as we enter, but the blackout blinds have been drawn and only splintered shafts of light cut across the thick darkness.

'Where's the light?' I ask, groping across the walls for the switch.

'No, wait,' he says. 'I want you to listen to this. It's important. It's the answer to... well... it's just the answer: *Art isn't about good artwork, but about being artistic. It's not about pretty pictures alone. It's about the attitude and sensitivities that a work of art may evoke. It's about giving the viewer something that they never could imagine* – Brad Greek.' There's a pause. He seems to require something from me, but I don't understand. 'Well,' he says, 'Don't you see? It's the fucking truth *and* the light.' I can hear it in his voice; he finds my lack of response irritating and I know that my place in the project relies on my engagement with this idea. I stall for time.

'Greek – he's the American guy who does that scratchboard art, right?' There's no response, he wants more. 'Oh, I see, Matt. You want to try something new...'

'It's more than that,' he interrupts. 'I need to make it new. Scrap this preoccupation with trying to capture the essence of things and shit. It's getting me nowhere anyway. I need a new angle; to start again with me, from within me. I'm going to produce a deconstructive study in my own deconstruction!'

He flicks the light switch. Standing in the middle of the room where the bed had previously been is a large cage on wheels. It's like one of those old-fashioned cages where they'd house circus animals in the Victorian times, elaborately carved and beautifully painted. It puts me in mind of a gypsy caravan, although it's only about two by one metres in size, with bars on four sides, a heavy wooden roof and straw on the floor. Matt waits – staring, panting. I close my eyes and slide slowly down the wall to the ground. 'What the hell...? Are you crazy?'

'I know. It's fucking magic, isn't it!' He dances around the cage rattling the bars, rocking it from side to side. 'This is it – my new piece. I already have a title: The Fasting Artist.'

'A what artist?'

'A fasting artist,' he says. 'They used to be really popular a few hundred years ago, travelling in circuses. You know, living in their cages, getting really thin and that. They were sideshow attractions along with the bearded ladies and other freaks, starving themselves in the name of art. That's where I got the idea for the circus cage. It all fits.' He pauses for a response.

I know that if I dismiss the idea he'll go ahead with it anyway, so I choose another tack. 'Well, you know it's not original,' I say. 'David Blaine did it a few years back, suspended in a glass box somewhere along the South Bank. It's just the same. You don't want it to look like an imitation of that, surely?' There's another silent space. I know Matt is carefully considering his argument. He begins to speak again, only this time he sounds more rational, more measured.

'Ah, yes, Blaine. But this is different. He did it for publicity, celebrity, sensationalism. I'll be fasting for *me*. I'll be purging, purifying, redefining myself; reconstructing the image. By becoming a living sculpture I can pare away the layers to reveal the truth. It'll be art that hurts!' He is watching me intently now, asking himself if I get it, if I'll be party to it. 'And as a study in deconstruction, if I'm the piece, you'll have to be the opposition, the artist as such, and then we'll bring the two elements together to show they're dependent on each other for their meaning. It's fucking visionary!' He comes over and sinks down next to me, puts his head in my lap and stares up into my face. 'Babe – you're my muse. You know it, *and* you're the only one who understands me; the only one I trust.' He sits up, clutches my face in his hands. I can smell the paint on his fingers as they press firmly into my cheeks. 'If you look deep inside yourself, deep, deep down, I know you'll be able to see it's the way forward for me... for us.' He is playing me now and although I feel both aroused and repulsed by the idea, I am drawn to its idealism. I take his hands from my cheeks, fold them into my own.

'I'm no artist, Matt. How will it work?'

'It's engagement in the process that matters,' he says quietly. 'The idea is that the two opposing objects will cancel each other out, causing the authority and autonomy of either opposite to be deconstructed.' I don't understand what this means, but I know he needs me and I want to please him. I push a strand of hair away from his eyes.

'You're a warped bastard, Matthew. You know that?' He smirks now, knowing that I will follow him. He wishes to begin immediately. He has thought carefully about this and made particular decisions regarding preparation. Stacked next to the crates of mineral water are large wicker baskets of lemons. His cameras, video equipment, brushes, paints and canvases are arranged on a scrubbed pine table, supported by a stack of enlightening texts to inform the work. It puts me in mind of a still life.

'I want you to take some photos of me every day so we can record the changes. And feel free to paint what you feel, what you see, your view of events as such. But no verbal communication, it might compromise the outcome.' I film him as he ceremoniously removes his clothes, climbs up onto the roof of the cage and enters through a small trap door. With a sigh, he settles himself into the straw, stretching out onto his back with his hands behind his head.

So it begins.

Matt languishes in the cage for the rest of the day. I settle myself on the chaise and watch. I watch the way his ribcage rises and falls and find my own breaths synchronised with each movement. I become transfixed by the way the slivers of sunlight send dappled winks across his skin. I notice a small diamond-shaped scar on the back of his calf; the way the hair that catches behind his ear turns and curls under his chin. I catch his subtle poetic shifts in posture on camera, print out the images and pin them onto the wall facing the cage. He nods approval. We do not speak, but still we know. He takes sips of water flavoured with fresh lemons. I carry away his waste in old jam jars.

At 7.00pm, he speaks: '*Art is an experience, not an object* – Robert Motherwell.' He dips his head towards me and puts a finger to his lips. After a significant pause, he sinks back into the straw and closes his eyes.

I awake on the second day with a start. I'd been dreaming I was in a refugee camp where hundreds of young children with huge rheumy eyes and grossly swollen bellies were all pushing against me, clamouring for food. I feel stiff and sore. The springs in the old chaise have made a chain of interlocking circular imprints along my thighs. I look over at Matt. He is lying on his side, propped up on one elbow, enjoying the view. 'You could've woken me. I was having a terrible dream.' He raises an eyebrow and pulls his mouth into a dimpled smile. 'Bastard!' I say.

We settle into the day. I take up some of the reading that Matt has collected together; books on philosophy, poetry, Deconstruction, Post-Modernism, and the texts soon urge me to reach out to him. 'You're certainly on the right track, Matt. Did you know that Yeats and Kafka both suggest that the creation of a work of art demands the deconstruction of the body?' His brow furrows. He will not acknowledge me and continues his silent contemplation of the cage ceiling.

Days three and four pass in much the same way. Matt is controlled. He now shuns all forms of communication. I look after things; eat snatches of meals in the bathroom. On the fifth day, I'm reading the works of Kahlil Gibran: *Art arises when the secret vision of the artist and the manifestation of nature agree to find new shapes.* I am compelled to share my discovery with Matt, who barely returns a dismissive shrug. I turn away, rub my eyes, massage a persistent throb at my temples.

The *secret vision*: the hidden truth maybe? The concept moves me and I feel the need for some sort of validation. The light in the studio is subdued on Matt's direction, in order that only shards of natural light will spotlight 'the piece'. I step up to the paints, take up a crusty palette and run my hands over the tubes. I squeeze out some oils – Raw Umber, Burnt Sienna, Yellow Ochre, Terre Verte – an earthy mix, not at all representative of the bright fairground colours of the cage. I dip broad flat brushes into the shining mounds of colour and apply it in bold strokes to a large blank canvas. I can see very little but I paint fast, piling on colour over colour, mixing and merging, without reference to the subject in front of me. I am half aware that Matt is standing up in the cage, craning his head to see what is happening, but I am working now and do not turn to him. A primitive form is emerging; a human figure, yes, with outstretched arms and large eyes, wide open.

I work urgently, without stopping to judge or criticise the strokes. The paint is thick, juicy, sexy, well suited to the softness of limb, sprawling of torso, rounding of breast. I can hear a metallic rattling, like something sharp being dragged along a radiator and am aware of a peripheral impression; an arm stretching towards me. But here in this space, I cannot be reached.

And then the white space is gone. A painting, heavy with itself, stands in its place. The bars of the cage make the imprisoned figure appear fragmented, spliced; dissected even. Perspective is accidental. I step away from the painting and turn to Matt. He turns away and sinks down on his haunches, hands forcing his head to his knees.

I slice some lemons and dilute their juices with water. I decant it into two cut glass jugs and drink hungrily from one, allowing the liquid to escape from my mouth and run down my chin. The other, filled to the brim, I tip over my head and stand dripping, shaking, screwing my eyes against the acidic burn, raking the lemon pips through my hair. Afterwards, I look back at Matt. He is on his haunches now, gripping the bars of his cage with both hands, peering between them with dark, shadowed eyes and I see that I am bored by his display of self-denial, his self-centred exhibitionism. He is angry and grimy and I notice that he is in fact, rather round-shouldered.

'Fucking bitch!' he growls. I turn on the light and take the canvas across to the cage. I reach up and remove one of his mirrors from its wire and replace it with the new painting, still shitting its colour. I stand back and review the complete piece:

'Deconstruction – within a successful work the two terms will cancel each other out in a mutual self-referencing so that all traditional oppositions are destabilised: good/bad, black/white, male/female, original/fake.'

'Meaning?' he grunts.

'You tell me, Matt. Something about truth and light maybe? Call me... or not.' Without looking back, I let myself out. I believe he is still squatting in the straw

Her name was Waggy, but really it wasn't. It was just one of those things. Danny Granger would always call his television remote the doodah. My sister and I would always call our dog Waggy. It was supposed to be Shettleston, and was, when she bit the heads off of our daffodils, messed on the tiles or had her head caught in a cereal packet. Otherwise it was Waggy; just one of those things that stuck. When she died, I went and stood in the garden and wouldn't go back inside. Waggy's body was in the kitchen, in her bed. My granddad said he would sort things. He set me to work on some gardening outside, pulling up vegetables. It was something to do.

He came out after lunch and I asked him if Waggy could be written on her gravestone. 'There won't be a grave,' my granddad said. 'It's too expensive and dogs don't have them.'

'What will there be then?' I asked.

'Wait there,' he said, and pointed to the pile of beetroot I had made. 'We'll get this done.'

Now, my granddad had two names as well, but we only ever used one. Not Granddad or Gramps – no one would ever call him that – it was Jock, even though his proper name, what came on the bills, was Philip. 'They called me Jock in the air force,' he told us. 'All the boys did because they were English, see?' We didn't see, but called him Jock anyway.

I was waiting by the beetroot pile when he came out with Waggy wrapped up in sheets. He placed her softly beside the old vegetable patch. 'Here,' Jock said, and passed me a carrot. 'It's been washed.' The carrots from the garden were never a good size or very straight-looking. They looked more like fingers or twigs, but I could always strip away the ugly outer carrot and leave the prickly spine until last. It would taste sweeter, the best part of it. Jock threw the other carrots he was carrying down onto the pile I had made. There were a good lot of vegetables on the lawn there – beetroot, carrots and cabbages – I assumed that Nan would be making some sort of a pie with them all in, and that we'd be having that for dinner, but this wasn't it. We were not using the vegetables. We were using the ground.

The patch I had been working on was barely the size of our living room, but with its ground all upturned, the soil mashed and frothy like dirty popcorn, I had never seen it look bigger or more plain. 'What now?' I asked.

'You don't have to work now,' Jock said. 'Go in to your Nan if you want. I'm gonna dig a hole here for Waggy-dog.'

'I don't want to go in,' I said. 'I'll watch.'

Jock went and fetched the shovel from inside. He didn't keep it in the shed, but in the pantry, because of yobbos. It was a good shovel, and safe there. As Jock dug the hole, I couldn't help but think that I could have done a better job if he had only let me. I may have only been twelve at the time and a weakling to boot, even for a twelve-year-old, but I could've held a spade like that without shaking it about all over the place. It looked as if Jock was fighting with it. His hands shook so much that great amounts of dirt would fall off the spade-head and back into the hole, even before he got it over his shoulder. He was filling the hole half as much as he was digging it. It wasn't the Parkinson's that made him shake. He didn't have that. 'It's oldness,' Nan once told me, 'just oldness.'

When I could only see Jock from the waist up, he stopped digging. I had been watching the heap of rags that covered Waggy this whole time. It wasn't moving, but when the wind blew the cloth tight to the shape of her back, I had to look away. It hadn't been our dog until then.

I went over and helped Jock out of the shallow ditch. He bent down towards Waggy and when he did I quickly went over to the beetroot pile again. Jock picked up the heap and laid it in the hole. That was it. It didn't take long to fill in what was dug out. When the ground was flat, I came over again to the old patch. 'It looks the same as it did before,' I said. 'Only there's no carrot tops poking through now. It's weird to think she's down there.' I looked at the earth. It was bare, quiet and ordinary; if earth could be those things. Jock had smoothed over a square in the mud where the hole had once been, but the rest of the ground still looked messy from where I had taken out the vegetables. It looked deep underneath, and having seen how far Jock had dug down, I knew it was. I knew Waggy was that deep, that far down. That was the closest I was to crying about it. Jock didn't cry either. He stood quietly for a long time before picking up the shovel again. 'A man should have an indoor passion and an outdoor one,' he said. 'That dog was my outdoor passion. I'll have to take you for walks now instead.'

'What's my outdoor passion?' I asked.

'I don't know. You dug up them vegetables pretty good. Now come on,' he said. 'Come inside.'

Jock left the vegetables where they were. For later, he said. We would fix them later.

The inside of our house would fill with smoke anytime Nan cooked food. She fried everything, otherwise grilled it, and the mist would rise high and above the first floor.

It pressed against the windows until you couldn't see in or out. It thickened, dirty grey smoke, and Nan would have to get me to reach the window latches and let it all out. 'It tests the fire alarms,' she would say. 'Keeps the batteries on their toes.'

'Can you die of the smoke?' I asked her that day.

'No,' she said. 'And don't you think it was that what killed her. That dog was old. She wasn't right.'

'Is it seven then?' I asked.

'What's that?'

'Five or seven, for dog years? I remember someone saying it was only five. That only makes Waggy seventy or so. Seventy exactly, actually. That's not old enough to be dying.'

'I'm seventy,' Nan said. 'Your granddad's seventy-two. You don't see us dying of the smoke or anything else.'

'That's because we can probably take more,' I said. 'It takes longer on us. The smoke could be giving Jock the shakes.'

'It isn't,' Nan said. 'And don't you go telling him that either. Don't go putting ideas in his head.'

'Why does he do it then? What do the doctors say?'

'Who knows?' Nan said. 'Mad the lot of them. You know what I think about doctors. You should think the same. I don't believe in them.'

Nan didn't believe in doctors the same way she didn't believe in lawyers or the French. 'A doctor's never done me any good,' she said, clearing dinner. 'Never did your dad no good neither. What good's a doctor in this day and age? It's all done with pills now anyway. You know, Dr. Buckley keeps changing his pills around. Jock went in the other day and the doctor said, 'The pills aren't working. Take these instead.' They bent his legs about and did tests. After all that bother that's all he came up with: new pills. So he's got them now, all in the morning as well. He takes four in the morning and that's it for the day. I don't know why they mess him about if they're supposed to know what they're doing. It'll be pills all over the place before they get it right.'

I believed her, but only because I knew how bad Jock could get. Carrying drinks was the worst, anything in a mug. They would call him 'half pint' down at the ex-serviceman's club because that's how much of his drink would be left in the glass by the time he got back to his seat. The rest would have dribbled onto the floor even if he held it in two hands. He couldn't write, he couldn't shave, he could barely get a fork to his mouth without cutting his lips. Still, he wasn't ill. He walked nearly ten miles a day. He could drive a car – he just couldn't stop shaking.

Jock was seventy-two, so Nan said. That would make him fourteen in dog years, but only ten if a dog year was seven. Dogs die at fourteen, so my dad used to say. I still don't know what a dog year is. I hoped it was seven though.

I didn't want to be in the same room as Waggy's old bed. Her water was there in the kitchen too, and her food tray. 'I'm going into the other room,' I told Nan. 'Can you get rid of this stuff?'

'Alright,' Nan said. 'Go and see Jock. He's in the chair.'

In the living room, there was 'the chair' and there was 'the settee' which was for two. There was 'the boofie' too, but that was to put your feet up. I could sit on the boofie as if it were a bench meant for sitting on. I could pull it close to Jock's chair and write the answers in the newspaper crossword for him. 'The standard detectives adhere to,' Jock read. 'What's that going to be? You should know that one.'

I looked up. Anytime we did the crossword, Jock would fold the paper in his lap and use a popped-out lens of an old magnifying glass to see the clues. 'I don't know,' I said. 'How many letters?'

'Nine. Blank, blank, r, then the rest blank.'

'I still don't know.'

'Yardstick,' Jock said, 'You should know that.'

I didn't understand, but wrote 'yardstick' in the space. I passed the paper back to Jock for the next clue, but he took it and put it aside without checking my spelling.

'That's enough done today,' he said.

Jock edged forward in the chair and looked as if he would try to stand up.

Instead, he reached behind the arm and pulled out his overnight bag. That bag hadn't been anywhere overnight for years, but Jock would never throw anything away. The original moonlight grey on it had faded, the edges chipped and battered, it held Jock's indoor passion and stayed buried away from where my Nan could find it, and hide it.

A banjo, I would always call it. It wasn't a banjo. 'Mandolin,' Jock would say. 'Man-do-lin. One of these days you'll remember it right.' The little instrument's wood panel was painted blue but you could still see the grain underneath, and a heart shape carved into the centre showed the thing was hollow. It was light. As light as a baby, and every time he would hand it to me I felt as I'd been given a baby. I would play a clumsy strum that rattled the wooden box before quickly giving it back. With me that was all it was; just a box with a neck with strings on. I could only make it sound ill, sound in pain – always coughing, clearing its hollows. Jock could make it sing. Let Mandy sing, he would say, and would take it back.

Jock rested the thing on his lap and fumbled for his song book. With shaking hands, he turned the pages. It would always be the same old songs. 'It's a long way to Tipperary' or 'Jerusalem.' It was a blues songbook really. Blues and Bluegrass for Mandolin, and every tune was familiar to me.

As Jock played, I watched his hands move fast and delicate, pinching the strings firmly where he needed, his eyes and head still. It sounded the sound I could never make, a song of practice that scared me just to witness it. I could tell Jock was good, and I wanted to be as good as him at something of my own. People would look at Jock and have something about him to hold onto; he was the guy with the little guitar. I wanted an indoor passion like that too, something quiet but impressive. More than that, I wanted Jock to explain something to me. 'How can you do that without shaking?' I asked. 'You can't dig a hole right or even have a shave, but you can do all that moving about on a banjo. Look at those tiny spaces that your fingers are meant for. If you can get that right then you can have a shave without killing yourself. It's not oldness, is it, Jock?'

'It's different to shaving,' he said.

'Because it's music?'

'No, nothing like that. It's just how I hold the neck here, see? I can hold onto a pole or a stick if its job is to stay still. I can hold a pen still. Look.' Jock gripped the crossword pen tight in his fist. He placed it down on a blank space in the personal ads and kept it perfectly still. I watched his hand intently, but not even his veins twitched. He lifted up the pen, his grip loosened, and his hands began trembling again. There was a solid dot on the paper now, proof that he hadn't shook at all, not even a shiver. 'Now watch this,' he said. Jock placed the pen back on the dot and started to draw a line. It started well, as straight as anyone could draw, but it began to wobble, the line bending, until Jock was shaking so much that the line broke off and started again, jittering along; he reached the end of the page and looked up at me. 'You see?' he said. 'Now I can't do that, can I?'

'I don't see why,' I said. 'You can move about on the banjo. You know where it all is, where you have to go. You don't shake to get there.'

Jock's expression answered me. He took a deep breath that steadied his head from bobbing around too much. At last he said, 'Don't think I'm going anywhere, will you? You know the doctors won't get me.'

'I know they won't,' I said. 'Take your pills though.'

'It's four in the morning. Four big ones, like great boiled sweets they are.'

'Do they stop the shaking?'

Jock didn't answer. He took my left hand in his, as if we were shaking on a deal, but Jock kept it there, not shaking at all. We were still. Then he pulled my hand towards him, stretching out my arm across the chair and his front. I thought at first that he wanted me to reach him something, but he didn't. He just held my arm out for a second and then let it go. I should have brought it back to me, but I let it rest there, hanging in the air, as Jock rummaged down the side of the chair for something else. I was in the vaccination pose kids and people do for nurses, and I half expected Jock to come up and jab me with some shot they had forgotten to give me as a baby. I looked away. 'Now let's try this,' Jock said.

When I looked back over, he had opened up the music book again and was tracking the pages back to the beginning of a song. When he had found what he wanted, he told me to look at the book. With my arm still laid out across Jock's front, he began to patter his fingers down upon my wrist. The first staves on the page were bare save for a few crotchets, an F, a C, a D. After just a few bars, I could tell that Jock was trying to play the song with nothing – just my arm. It was odd at first. His hand skipped over the length of my sleeve as if the stitching guided him. His nails drummed lightly on my elbow and my veins and as the notes on the page formed closer groups, the song building – his thumb gripped the back of my hand and came over my watch – I could feel it pressing, steadying his whole arm. 'Am I shaking now?' he asked.

'No,' I said. 'You're playing it good and still.'

The notation thickened on the second page, the scales stamped with semiquavers and quick changes. Jock's fingers raced accordingly and for the most part, I think I could follow. 'That's it,' Jock said. 'Now, can you sing it?'

'I don't know the tune,' I said. 'Can't you sing?'

Without answering, Jock began on some words. It was a slow song at first. Each syllable took such a time to sing that I barely caught the meaning of a full word. It was something about hills. Someone was rambling. 'He kept on rambling,' Jock sang. The word came up over and over. Jock went on playing the notes on my arm as he would on the mandolin, measured and delicate. He never shook. Nan could hear the singing and came in from the kitchen. 'What's all this racket?' she said. 'Jock, let go of him. What are you playing at?'

I didn't answer. 'We're playing at this song,' Jock said. 'I'm teaching him here.'

Nan said something else. Whatever it was, I let it ring numb in my ears. I could hear nothing but the quiet patter of a mandolin that wasn't being played, that wasn't even there. I didn't know the song in the book, the rambling song – thought I knew them all, but as Jock mimed its rhythm, it was like hearing nothing I'd ever heard him play before. I say hearing, but I don't know what it was. I closed my eyes and let the slowness take me. All the while, he never shook.

Afterwards, Jock sent me to the kitchen to clear plates. I did the job quietly, and was quiet for some time after that. I went back out into the garden and looked at Waggy's grave and the pile of vegetables on the lawn. I didn't know whether those vegetables were dead or alive, whether or not they'd grow again if I planted them, but it was something to do. I started planting in rows, as they were before: carrots on the left, beetroot, then cabbage on the right. The ground was hard in the evening air, the garden fork cold, its prongs blunt and dirty. I dug a hole, put something in it, and closed the hole. I spent a good deal of time patting down earth around each of the stems until I couldn't see the main part of each thing. I buried the cabbages right underground. It wasn't my outdoor passion, but it was a job. I stood back and looked at the stems coming through the ground. It was something now, that vegetable patch.

I would go back there often, long after I moved out of my grandparents'. It was years later, even many dog years later, but I would still get the mandolin out from its case from time to time and play that same clumsy strum of mine. It angered me that I could never be as good as Jock, but at least the banjo was safe. At least it was mine; that one thing I had always asked him to leave to me in the will. Just the banjo, I would say. He left me his house of course, the banjo too. 'Mandolin,' he would always say. 'One of these days you'll remember it right.'

The car is propelled from the roundabout like a lunar module thrown from orbit and we hurtle into the darkness of space. No streetlights line this small country wormhole, only lines of cats' eyes slicing the road into three. Reflective red hems in each edge, a dotted white incision carving the middle. Comrade James, sitting on my right, guides the vessel through. We're space invaders wavering on a dark screen; perforated streams of missiles hurtling towards us at the speed of light. The car gobbles the cat's eyes as it glides bravely ahead and I imagine a little points counter on the dash sliding up and up.

'I feel like Pac-Man,' says James, his thoughts running typically parallel to mine. 'Put some better music on.'

Admittedly, Bob Dylan telling everyone they must get stoned doesn't quite fit the surroundings as well as it did a moment ago – we were humming along fine, happy in the electric orange comfort of a well-lit motorway at night, my bare feet up on the front window. I remember noticing sand was still between my toes. Now I'm upright, alert, clammy. My thighs stick to the faux-leather seat and my dress sticks to me. It's exciting to drive in such darkness but James has just passed his test and he's cocky. He never slows down. I worry about shadows scurrying out onto the tarmac, of night creatures caught under merciless wheels.

To take my mind off the road, I follow his request and pick up the Mp3 player plugged into the car stereo. Cutting off Bob mid-groan, I tap at the little central button glowing a tiny inscription – *select*. A word that comes with a promise. I press it fervently, searching for a song to match our new surroundings. So much music to be savoured. The air between us fills with incomplete beginnings: guitars that crash to a halt, drums that suddenly collapse, singers whose voices are pinched into silence. We punctuate each lull between tracks with our own chorused rejections: 'No... No... Not that... Abba?' 'Definitely not...' and the quest continues.

With the music library set to random it's a longer process, but a silent understanding between us dictates that this must be the way it's done. We don't want to find the perfect song. We want to discover it. We want it to strike out at us like a lightning bolt setting a forest on fire. Nothing draws me closer to James than this. The simultaneous spark of recognition that marks the end to a search for the perfect piece of music.

We often play games like this. We ask each other: if this was a film, what would the soundtrack switch to at this moment? What could possibly elevate this tiny segment of our insignificant little lives and make it something worth paying attention to? The answer has always been music, a thread that binds us and unravels backwards in time, as early as five, when we danced around my garage on a rainy afternoon to my father's

Travelling Wilburys tape, played at full volume and echoing off the leaky aluminium roof.

'Keep this on,' says James suddenly, the corner of his mouth turning up. A grinding guitar riff fills our small space of air and a low growl booms all around. The artist selected is Death in Vegas, the song 'Aisha', and he's right, the music is pounding and creepy and guttural enough for a dark drive into the unknown. I look through the window to my left. It's completely black. Leaning back against the cold glass, I block it out. Perhaps this music is a little *too* atmospheric. James doesn't share the sentiment. He loves stuff like this. When I was younger, when he last knew me, I did too.

We lived next door to each other; he was my surrogate twin for seventeen years. After we finished college, we decided to take a gap year before going to university. For a few weeks, the freedom was intoxicating. Then, it was simply a background hum. Then, it became plain dull. To me, anyway. I think James was still having the time of his life sitting on his bed all day, strumming a guitar, a habit which confused and eventually infuriated me.

One day, same as ever, we were lying on his bed listening to an old psychedelic record from the 60s, when I found myself zoning out to the map of the world sellotaped to his wall. He'd put it up about ten years back, when we'd gone through a When I Grow Up phase of wanting to become explorers. That lasted a few months, abandoned later for astronauts, but the poster remained, clinging by a few curls of sellotape. As if in a trance, I got up, picked a pin off his desk and stuck it into a section of the glossy card. I don't even remember where it was. It didn't matter. It was somewhere else.

'I want to travel!' I said, turning to him with what he described later as a terrifying smile. 'James, let's go, let's do it... if we save enough, we can.'

He agreed, haltingly, then proceeded to save no money at all for six months while I worked at a coffee house and a call centre and talked to him incessantly about where we might go, and how we might get there. When the day came to go to the travel agent, he walked halfway with me before he broke the news. I was so angry I stormed off and booked a single ticket, just to spite him. The next day, waking up in a cold sweat, feeling untethered, I rushed back to cancel the flights, balking at the cancellation fee. I was caught. I was going to the other side of the world, whether I liked it or not.

When I returned a year later – tanned and mosquito-bitten and completely and utterly happy – I was wearing a turquoise tunic-dress. I bought it in New Zealand because it matched the colour of the sea. Meeting me at the airport, James held me at arms length and said, 'So, you're wearing *dresses* now?' before hugging me in a way I didn't like. This was my welcome back to England. This was the month at home before University began.

So I wore the dress again today, perhaps a little defiantly, perhaps a little abashed, to our annual last-hot-day-of-summer beach trip. We did the things we always did: ate chips on the beach, paddled in the still-cold sea, went on the dodgems in Funland with sandy seats. I talked about looking down at the Himalayas from my aeroplane. He talked about buying a second-hand car and starting a new band. Somehow, the conversation fitted together. The only moment I remembered we'd changed was when he rolled the towel across to me and said, 'I bet this beats anything that happened on your great travels,' and planted a self-assured kiss on my shoulder. And there it remained, like a new creature released into civilisation – something I couldn't catch and stuff back in its cage. It still perches there, and I remember it every few minutes or so.

James is unaware of this new presence. His eyes are on the road but his head is full of rhythm and chords. The car swallows up the cats' eyes faster than ever. We approach a corner and he swerves too quickly, throwing me into his arm, then back against the window. My seatbelt creaks. The voice in the stereo booms '…I'm a murderer,' and I feel instantly panicked. Suddenly, I don't want to be inside this car at all.

'James, slow down,' I squeak.

My mind is running as fast as the car. I see dots of light blurring into one long line and silvery air battering up the windscreen like backwards-flowing water. I imagine a new heat buzzing against the hairs on my arms and its source becomes immediately clear: an overcooked engine, corroded parts of machinery all whirring and snapping bits off one another, any semblance of our control over the vehicle degrading to scrap. A corner looms ahead and I know already what's going to happen; that we'll cut our own path through the darkness, cross the red boundary of the road's edge and smack straight through the great reflective arrow that indicates right.

'Slow the fucking car down!'

My voice is a shockwave. It severs the music in half and pierces James's own thick skin with the precision of an arrow. I see him jump. His fingers disjoin from the wheel, his knees lift from their crook. He turns to me in an instant this time, and his face is completely altered by my words. It's as if I've reached inside him and yanked at the hanging wires. He's become all disconnected. I can see his glow fade. The car duly slows to a respectable pace; the corner is rounded perfectly.

'I think I need Dylan back,' he says, after a beat. 'Change the song.'

I comply. The speakers blossom new sounds between us. We sit awkwardly, trapped in the prickly presence of each other's disapproval. I make a play list of all his favourites, but my attempt to heal the atmosphere misfires. 'Like a Rolling Stone', 'Baby Blue' and 'Mr. Bojangles' just remind us of the good times we had in their company, and, consequently, only serve to highlight the rotten time we're having right now. I scrunch into my seat. I realise what was in his face now – a realisation, a new flow of unwanted knowledge that told him we weren't so alike anymore. This thought digs into me, and all I want is to take James's hand off the steering wheel and hold it, for a little while, in mine. But, of course, I don't, and then the next junction looms into view and the moment to seize an opportunity passes.

We escape the primeval dark of the little road and make a half-circle of the new roundabout, blinking through the glare of a halo of streetlights. We take the road straight upwards and we're back on another motorway. A nice, artificially bright and speedy place, hopefully enough to perform some kind of osmosis upon the gloom within the car.

'Nearly home!' I say merrily. The first words I've spoken in a while.

'We've still got an hour to go,' he replies with a slight sneer.

I have no quick comeback in store. I would have had a year ago, and we'd have been off, insults becoming more disgusting and outrageous until one of us broke the charade and collapsed into laughter. But I don't know what to say to him any more. I don't know what's okay. Now, the silence lingers.

'Look,' he says in a softer tone. 'Look...' he says again, struggling a little, catching my eye, looking back at the road, looking back at me. We pass a sign. Fifty miles until home.

'What is it?' I say. I try to be cool, to intimidate him for once, but my body betrays me and I lean into the gap between us. A strand of my hair escapes, brushing his bare arm.

He falters. 'Fifty miles, should be less than an hour now. Hey, change the song will you?'

I rest back in my seat. Sighing, picking up the Mp3 player, I begin to press *Select*...

When Mrs Dhali came from Dhaka to Manchester Coach Station on an unseasonably mild October day, she told herself she had no idea why she'd come. A few days before, she'd announced to her husband, in quite a severe voice, that they should both go to England for a visit. She spoke to him in a way that suggested he might like to book the flight tickets immediately, although she knew very well he was tied up in a series of important meetings all that day and the next. When he confirmed this in his soft, measured voice, she simply said, 'Very well, I will book them myself.' She didn't tell him she had the tickets in her bag already, along with their new thin passports.

She watched her husband flutter around over the next few days like a disturbed bird who was about to be thrust from his nest. She bought his favourite boiled sweets and tucked them into the corner of the bag with the passports and the tickets. She bought a whistle and put that in too because she'd heard that whistles could be useful in England. She packed thick sweaters for her husband and thin cashmere cardigans to wear in layers under her sari, if necessary.

On the day before departure, she paid a visit to the biggest store in the city; the one frequented by many foreigners. She bought several items for herself and a tweed jacket for her husband with six matching cotton shirts and two dark woollen ties. She also bought three matching black cases. Each case was larger than the next. The largest had wheels and a handle for easy transport. She spent a long time in the jewellery department and selected two gold chains for her reading glasses. She went to the book department, walking up and down the aisles, peering at the shelves of books for a long time until she found what she wanted. A coffee-table book on the 'Railway Locomotives of England'. She arranged for all the parcels to be delivered at her house the following day.

That night, she told her husband the arrangements had been made. He thanked her rather formally and they sat down to a light dinner, prepared by Mrs Dhali (she always prepared and cooked their food herself despite having a cook) in the unhurried, thorough way that her mother had taught her, before switching on the television for the evening's viewing. Later, they both went to their separate rooms and passed the night alone.

Mrs Dhali always read for a while but this night she sat up in bed without a book. She heard her husband opening and closing doors, and switching off the main light and finally, after the usual ten minutes, she heard the click of the bedside lamp and the fall of the book as it hit the floor. She sat in the cool bed with the starched cotton sheets and she sat like that for a long time looking out at the dark, cloudy night where everything was tinged with yellow from the street lights.

In the time between the end of night and the beginning of day, she left her bed and sat on a chair at the window. She could see things better in that half-light where all things crept out so easily it was as though they'd been waiting for her. She listened to the sounds they made, the squeaking of brakes on the rickshaw bicycles as the paper boys began their rounds, the shuffling of the first trains as they slowed into the nearby Dhaka station, reluctant to pull at their engines fully until they had to, and the quick high cry of the wild cats who circled the city. She sat at the window and when the first express train came through without stopping, when she heard the thick whistle blow three times in warning, she stood up and reached out to hold a little of its speed in her hands and held it there for a moment, then released it to go where it was going, until the next time.

The morning after, she made pancakes for breakfast filled with sweet fruits like lychees and dried coconut pieces dipped in sugar. She laid them on a plate ready to eat when her husband came. She saw his surprise at once, and his pleasure as he ate the warmed pancakes and sipped at the sweet milky tea. 'Tomorrow we will go,' she said. She saw how his hands trembled as he placed the thin cup on the saucer. Like a bird who is afraid, she thought. A tenderness touched her for a moment as she acknowledged his fear. 'We will be fine,' she said. 'There are many interesting things to see in England. We'll be the wiser afterwards.'

Her husband looked at her with his soft brown eyes as though he wanted to speak about something that lay beyond him, but he only said, 'Of course. There is much to see. We will go to all the places of finance. I will learn something there.' He wiped sugar from his lips, rinsed his hands, and when the driver rang the door bell, he waited with his briefcase for the day ahead.

Mrs Dhali left the clearing of the kitchen to Sita, the young girl who came in every day to help, and began her preparations for their departure. First, she laid out their travelling clothes. For her husband, the new tweed jacket and a dark blue shirt and one of the black ties. She hung them, with a dark pair of trousers, on his wardrobe door. Then she laid out her best sari, dark pink with pale orange streaks like a sunset over the River Ganges. As a little girl she'd once walked with her father along its banks. They'd seen a wooden raft drifting downstream with garlands of flowers over it. Her father told her someone had died and would soon be going to a different place. She remembered the colours and how the pink sky had whispered to her that one day she would come closer and see how the colours of pink and orange could lie across the water like a giant bridge to a special place. She'd asked her father if they could go there but he was silent for a long time. Just when she thought he hadn't heard her, he lifted her up and held her over the waters so she could watch the raft until the very last moment, until the flowers shone in the water and waved to her.

Mrs Dhali packed strong sturdy shoes for walking. She'd heard that there were many places for walking in England. Then she wrote out in large letters, with a thick pen: DHAKA TO MANCHESTER COACH STATION and taped the notice onto each suitcase with thick white tape, the type used in hospitals and sold in the markets because it was strong and the glue wouldn't weaken. She took a bath and washed her long black hair and waited through the day for it to dry. Before her husband came home, she plaited it and secured it in a low neat bun on her head with the gold clips she'd received on her wedding day, the day she'd met her husband for the first time. Everything was gold on that day. It had shone so much her eyes were full of it, so full they could scarcely see her new young husband who'd journeyed from another region. 'You will be happy,' her mother and father had told her. 'You will get to know him very quickly. You will learn what he likes and what he dislikes. You will be happy.' She'd worn her gold bangles and a red and green sari with gold threads. She'd been happy. She was glad to have been betrothed to such a handsome young man when she was young. She learnt how to be a wife quickly. She learnt how to be a mother more slowly, but once she had learnt, the learning stayed inside her and became part of her.

She left the book on locomotives wrapped in the paper from the store and then she packed it carefully in with the other smaller items: jewellery, basmati rice, a small box of cardamom seeds and dried saffron, although she'd heard you could buy these things in England.

That evening, she told her husband about her preparations. He thanked her and they ate the meal she had prepared; a mild curry that he always enjoyed. After the meal he couldn't settle to television watching, even though it was his favourite programme on Channel 'I'. He walked up and down the room several times before saying good night and going to his room. Mrs Dhali followed him upstairs and went to her own room. Again, she didn't read, but waited until the night began outside her window. She joined it where the thick heat met the heavy smells of the day gone before, always with the smooth hard light from the yellowing street lamps that swept over the city. In the half-light between night and day, she left her bed and bent forward in her chair until the familiar sounds whispered to her, stroking her and bringing her comfort.

In the morning, they waited with their cases for the car which would take them to the airport. Mrs Dhali straightened her husband's neck tie, just as a wife should before such a journey. On the plane they both slept, keeping their dreams apart.

It was six o'clock in the evening when Mr Dhali carried the cases from the shuttle bus into Manchester Coach Station. Mrs Dhali hurried after him pushing the larger case in front of her. She panted with the effort and the bottom of her sari kept catching in the wheels. She grunted several times as they moved slowly in the queue of people heading for the exit. 'We will need a taxi,' she said to her husband. 'We cannot walk like this to the station.' She held out a small map she'd obtained at the airport where two red crosses marked the coach station and the railway station. The words, YOU ARE HERE , were written next to the coach station.

'It is not far,' her husband said. 'We do not need a taxi.'

She shouted at him. 'I will not walk like this. Go from here and find a taxi.' She shook her arm and the gold bracelets clashed like cymbals. 'I will stay here with the cases.' She sat on a small metal bench turning her head this way and that and muttering to herself in her childhood language of Bengali. Mr Dhali hovered around her arranging her sari carefully on the floor and pushing the cases closer around her until she felt like a rare species sitting in a cage at the zoo. She shouted at him again. 'Never mind the cases. Get a taxi. Can't you do it?' He stood back with great calmness and looked at her. When he was sure she was settled in the correct manner, he walked over to the automatic doors and passed through.

Mrs Dhali sat on the bench for a long time, sweating. She wished she hadn't put two cardigans on under her sari. She was surprised at the heat in England. The ex-patriots she'd met at the Sheraton Hotel in Dhaka had spoken of the coldness of their country. All the books spoke of cold but she wasn't cold now. Sweat was running down her back.

A group of teenage girls gathered in front of her. Mrs Dhali was tired and irritated. She wanted to tell them to go away. She held her silence for a while, watching as more girls joined the group, this time with pushchairs holding one, sometimes two babies. Her irritation grew. Where are their mothers? To leave their babies with such schoolgirls. It made her feel crosser still now she could see nothing in front of her except the ever-increasing group of girls. Some young men joined them. They were wearing white jogging suits and white training shoes and white caps pulled forward on their cropped heads. They spoke loudly in front of her. Her head began to throb in a familiar way; first the jabbing pain just above the top of her spine, then the slow moving throb to the right side of her head through her right eye, like a well-practised form of abuse. She sat up straight and called out in a voice neither high nor low but one she judged would be heard effectively. 'Go away.'

A girl dressed in a short skirt made of shiny material, holding a baby under her arm, looked at Mrs Dhali directly in the eyes. Mrs Dhali could see the black pupils focussing on her like a vulture eyeing up prey, intent on taking it apart, piece by piece, to chew for a while and then discard. She remembered a family picnic when she was young and how the vultures had sat on the branch of a tree, waiting and watching with dark eyes until one of them had swooped down and taken the meat from her fingers. She remembered the fear which lasted for a long time.

The girl moved her gaze away slowly, at the last minute staring hard before turning back to chat with the other girls. Mrs Dhali sat back on the bench, suddenly breathless. The noise continued. Now it was all around her as a new group moved into the coach station from another airport bus.

The loudspeaker system announced delays due to unexpected fog. Mrs Dhali tried again, summoning up anger as she repeated her earlier demand, this time adding another word, to indicate status. 'Go away. Immediately.' She knew as soon as the words left her mouth that they would not be heard in such a commotion. She stood up with difficulty amidst the cases and used her highest voice with a new, sharp anger in it, pointing her bangled arms at the group. 'Go away immediately!' One of the young men heard her and gestured to the others. She saw them all turn. A glance passed between them, linking them, holding them together as they raised their arms in unison and moved as one towards her. Mrs Dhali stood there breathing in a strange way. One part of her breath felt as though it had left her body too soon, the other as though it was stacked up inside her, choking her. She watched the hands and fingers pointing and jabbing the air, building to a crescendo of movement, like a tidal wave threatening to drown her. Slowly, she let her arms fall to her side. She could hear the soft tinkling of her gold bangles as they slid down her arm. All the time their eyes watched her, their voices shouting in unison, shaking their white arms at her. 'Go away,' they shouted. 'Go away immediately.' The roar of their voices held her in it and she began to tremble and shake as though she were part of an earthquake. She moved her hand to find something to steady herself with, but there was nothing. She swayed and they roared again, and then they were laughing until they were bending down in front of her, choking now with the new hard laughter spilling from them. Then, as suddenly as they had begun it, they finished it and turned away with indifference.

Slowly, Mrs Dhali felt her way down onto the bench and put her hands out to touch the cases one by one around her. She arranged her sari smoothly over her knees which trembled. She felt smaller, as though she had shrunk. She was shivering, waiting in the new coldness.

'Are you coming?' said her dead daughter busily pulling off the children's coats and folding the double buggy up. Mrs. Dhali didn't answer. She was so cold it was difficult to get her lips to move into any position for speech. Her daughter was chatting just the way she always used to. 'It's taken you a long time to come.'

Mrs Dhali thought before she spoke. 'I used to take you to the park every day when you were little. The best park in Dhaka.'

Her daughter smiled affectionately. 'I know you did. You don't think I've forgotten.' She pushed Mrs Dhali into a brightly coloured cushioned chair in front of the fire. 'You still look cold. Hold the baby and I'll make her the bottle and get you a hot drink'.

Mrs Dhali felt the soft heaviness of the baby on her knee and smelt its unfamiliar smell. She watched as her daughter put the other child into a high chair and placed diluted juice in a Peter Rabbit beaker and gave it to him.

Mrs. Dhali said, 'You're lucky to have one of each.'

Her daughter chuckled at the sink. She was mixing dried milk in a jug.

'It's hard work.' She poured the milk into a bottle and put it into the microwave. She pressed the 40-second switch. 'You don't know how easy you had it.' Her daughter laughed again as she took the baby off Mrs Dhali's knee and tied a bib around its neck. 'Do you want to feed her?' Without waiting for an answer, she put her back on Mrs. Dhali's knee. 'You have to hold her upright and make sure there's no air in the bottle.' She screwed the rubber teat on and tipped the bottle over the back of her hand so that the milk dripped onto her skin. 'That's perfect,' she said and handed the bottle over. Mrs. Dhali took it nervously. She held it near the baby's mouth. Her daughter laughed. 'You have to put it into her mouth. She's not old enough to find it! Come on Grandma, this is your chance.' And then her dead daughter went out of the room.

Mrs Dhali sat in the quiet room by the window with the baby and the bottle. She was warmer now. The sound of the smooth regular sucks as the baby drank the milk and emptied the bottle made her feel sleepy. She wondered if her husband had found the taxi yet. She felt anxious about the luggage she had left unattended. She would ask her daughter what to do about it. It didn't seem responsible to just leave it there. She thought of the book she had brought with her and how carefully she had packed it. How surprisingly heavy it had seemed in the suitcase. She felt her eyes close and in her drowsiness she could hear the sound of a locomotive, its pistons churning like a lament, filling her ears. She longed to stretch out to it but her hands were filled with other things now and she could only listen and wait as it passed through her onto the next part of its journey. The part she knew well. It reverberated in her head and she remembered when her mother had told her its story for the first time; when she, Mrs Dhali, was already big with her own daughter.

'Beware the locomotives,' her mother had told her and now Mrs Dhali hears again the sound of her mother's voice piercing her like shafts of light through closed shutters. 'They come and they take,' her mother said, and in her sleep Mrs Dhali stirs restlessly knowing only too well what her mother wants her to hear again. 'Listen,' she tells her. 'Listen to the sound of the Dhaka Express. It is coming.'

Mrs Dhali hears the familiar sound of the locomotive, growing louder like a wall being built from nothing, on nothing until it stands swaying and high enough to topple and crush all that lies beneath it.

'Listen to the crowds,' her mother said. Mrs Dhali listens and watches as the crowds of men swarm from the inside and the outside of the small train from the suburbs, like bees disturbed from their nest by a giant hornet. She sees them jumping down onto the tracks to cross over to the other side where they will arrange their baskets of small things to sell to the people of Dhaka. She sees how their sweat stains the white dhotis and how the heat holds itself over them, thickly, like an omen which is dark and full of heaviness.

And Mrs Dhali cried out, 'But what of the Dhaka Express?' And her mother said what she knew she would say. 'Ah, but they don't hear the sound of its coming. And how it is hidden there. Listen. Can you hear it?' Mrs. Dhali listens and at first she can't hear and then a sound comes that rises in the air, that presses hard against it, taking the breath from it and pushing that terrible speed ahead, until Mrs Dhali is moaning, moaning as she sleeps, seeing the sight of her own tears falling. 'No, no,' she screams. But it is too late. It is too late.

'Listen to the sound of the wheels,' her mother said and Mrs Dhali holds her hands across her ears to block out the sounds of the wheels which roar through, breaking everything in their path, spreading it carelessly, like debris from the city abattoir.

'Listen to the sounds,' her mother said and Mrs Dhali listens to the silence that flutters and stops. She sees the women who come, who bend and crouch low to gather it in their arms, who walk up and down the sides of the track for a long time and then, finally, she sees how they stand together, each in their own space, waiting, like thin reeds on the river bank, until they are ready.

Mrs Dhali felt herself jerk upright as the baby's bottle hit the floor. Her hands had loosened and now the baby was not held but was lying quietly at an angle across her knees. I might have dropped her, she thought and the baby's gaze seemed to fix on her as though she was berating her in some way. Mrs Dhali felt uncomfortable. In the distance, she could hear Mr Dhali. 'There is no taxi yet,' he called out and she heard the same slight trembling in his voice.

Was I too proud? she thought. But who wouldn't be too proud. There were principles at stake. It was about doing the right thing.

'But was it the right thing?' she said out loud, and watched as the baby first rubbed one eye with a fist, then moved the fist down jamming it into the open mouth, sucking at it energetically. Mrs Dhali wished again that her daughter had listened and come home to Dhaka as planned, when her studies at the University in London had been concluded.

'You will get a good job here,' Mr Dhali had told her on the telephone, and later in his letters written on the old Imperial typewriter and signed in a neat, fine flourish. Now Mrs Dhali thought about shame. It seemed to her a very shameful thing when a daughter discarded the old ways. 'Come home,' she had said to her. 'There is your husband-to-be to consider.' She was shocked at the way her daughter had laughed, as though she had said something amusing. 'I won't marry a man I don't know. I will marry the man I love.' Mrs Dhali remembered the brightness that shone in her words like a warning, and how she had telephoned her and asked her once again to come home, but her daughter said she could not and would not, because she had fallen in love with an Englishman and she was going to marry him in the English way, and then she didn't ask her again. 'We will not visit,' she said and then she let a kind of wailing rise up inside her and she kept it there for a while until she was pale and thin with it until finally, one day, she pushed it down deep inside so that it was almost forgotten. Mr Dhali never spoke of it again but she saw how he was changed. There was an emptiness in him, like a dying that couldn't be ended.

Mrs Dhali wanted a cup of tea. The boy in the high chair had finished his drink and was banging his cup up and down on the plastic surface. She felt her head beginning to throb again. Then the baby on her lap began to scream and kick her legs hard. Mrs Dhali looked at her. Briefly, she wondered if there was something she should be doing to stop the screaming and banging. She decided instead to concentrate on the type of tea she would choose when her daughter came back. She preferred a light tea in the afternoon served in a thin porcelain cup on a saucer, with two slices of lemon. She waited and the night came slowly and filled the room with its thickness. The baby cried herself to sleep on her knee and the little boy rocked backwards and forwards in his chair, calling, 'Mummy, mummy, mummy,' and banging his head on the wall behind the chair until Mrs Dhali thought she would go mad with the noise of it all. 'Be quiet,' she said but her voice was tired. 'She will come soon,' she said, but he screamed and shouted until his face was wet and red.

'Of course she will,' said her daughter carrying a tray with cups and saucers, a small teapot and a plate of thinly sliced lemon. 'She will always come.'

'You've been a long time,' said Mrs Dhali. 'I was beginning to think you would never come.' Her voice was petulant like a child who'd been deprived of a promised treat.

Her daughter laughed and took the baby off her knee. 'Goodness,' she said. 'This nappy needs changing and the breakfast things need washing up and the washing needs hanging on the line outside and he..,' she nodded in the direction of the little boy, 'he needs bathing and getting dressed in clean clothes and then he needs to be taken to nursery and the house needs cleaning and he needs picking up again and then the lunch needs to be cooked but first the shopping needs to be done and then...'

Mrs Dhali interrupted her. 'I'd like a cup of tea,' she said, using her slightly haughty voice. As she spoke, the night seemed to come like a heavy cloud covering everything in darkness. She felt the pain in her head spreading through her until she ached with it and longed to open the windows and hear the sounds of the locomotives which passed beneath her so she could hold them in her hands and cherish them. But all she heard was the sound of her dead daughter laughing.

'When I grow up I want to be a train driver,' she'd said one day when the rains had arrived. They were sitting outside on the wooden veranda, waiting for Mr Dhali to come home. On the table in front of them was a pile of old National Geographic magazines which Mrs Dhali's mother sent every month. The pages were soft and damp and easily torn. Everything was marked by humidity.

'I like the way they take you from one place to another place,' the little girl had said. 'Like magic.' She held up a magazine showing a picture of the railway in Dhaka. Mrs Dhali leaned forward in her chair. 'That's an old picture,' she said. 'I'll take you to see the big new locomotives that go so fast you think you're flying.'

'I'd like to fly in a fast train,' her daughter said, reading slowly the words, 'The Railway System in England' that were set under a colour photo of three newly acquired locomotives. She pointed at each word carefully and when she came to the word England, she repeated it and said, 'I want to go to England and marry a prince and stay there.' She traced the outline of the train with her finger. 'And I'll have a palace right next to the railway so that I can keep my train in the palace garden.' When Mr Dhali came home she ran to him and he lifted her high in the air and swung her around until she squealed with laughter, and then she begged to be put down again and pulled him to the table, showing him the brightly coloured pictures of the locomotives. Then she told him of her plans and Mrs Dhali said nothing.

'You'll have to find the prince here and build your palace in Dhaka so we can visit,' said the father.

'Of course I will,' the little girl said as though there was no question about it at all. 'But I'll go to England first.' And Mr and Mrs Dhali smiled at each other as if in agreement.

Mrs Dhali looked at her daughter who was dressed in a thick camel coat and sturdy boots and a bright scarf made of silk. 'Is it that cold?' she said, thinking of how warm she was on arrival.

'The weather changes quickly here,' her daughter said, putting the baby into a zip-up coat and fur-lined boots.

Mrs Dhali noticed how her face was pale now and there were deep dark rings under her eyes. 'You look like you need more sleep,' she said, and she shifted a little stiffly on the chair, glad the baby had gone from her knee. Her daughter didn't reply as she unfolded the pushchair with one hand and secured the lock on it. Then she put the baby in the seat on the right hand side and pulled her arms into the straps and clicked the buckle shut. Mrs Dhali heard her sigh deeply, saw tears running down her face, and she recognised them and remembered the time when the same tears had run down her own face, lining them; but then they were unseen.

'Where's your husband?' she said suddenly. But there was silence all around and a new darkness came which blinded her for a time which was neither long nor short. She sat in the darkness and waited. She listened for the sounds of the trains pulling out of the station so that she could hold them carefully and learn what she needed to know, but there was nothing there. Only the silence which stood in a circle around her, keeping her within it.

'My husband's there,' said her daughter, pointing into the distance where the light seemed to move in and out of a strange dimness. 'Can't you see him? Sitting in the big room watching the football on the television like he always used to.'

Mrs Dhali looked. 'I can't see anyone,' she said crossly, but her daughter continued as though she hadn't spoken.

'Look at him. See how he's laughing and clapping his hands. See how he drinks his beer until he sleeps. See how happy he is.' And the little boy began to laugh and clap his hands too and Mrs Dhali's daughter cried out happily, 'Yes, That's right. That's right.' And she laughed and pirouetted around him as she clapped her own hands as loudly as possible, all the while tears running down her face. Then her face thinned and became dark with her loneliness and the baby smiled and gurgled and kicked her legs and waved her chubby arms in the air.

Mrs Dhali was reminded of a play she had seen at the Dhaka Playhouse where the characters had to prove how happy they were, and they clapped, sang and danced until they had nothing left except themselves, and then the audience learnt the truth. She saw her daughter still laughing and dancing and clapping with her children until they were covered in the darkness that let no one in.

'The taxi's here,' Mr Dhali said.

'But you haven't said hello. You haven't said goodbye,' their daughter called out.

'We would like to,' said Mr Dhali, 'but it's too late. We haven't got time.' Mrs Dhali noticed how he struggled to keep his voice strong.

'What about the children?' their daughter said. Her voice was fading and the sound of a train could be heard approaching. 'They would love to play with you. Please stay and play with them.' Her words seemed to fly from a place where the wind was wild and strong, begging them.

'We haven't got time,' said Mr Dhali, his voice hurried and deliberate. 'We are from Dhaka. We must return there. Perhaps another time.' He lifted the cases into the boot of the taxi clumsily so that one was caught on the side of the boot and the clasp was wrenched open. Mrs Dhali watched him trying to close it again, failing. He took the case out impatiently and left it on the pavement. She could see the book she had packed lying on top and the whistle and the shoes and now she knew she didn't need them anymore because now she knew why she had come to this place. She knew that Mr Dhali had always known. She saw him shiver as he got into the front seat of the taxi and peered at the crowds, looking for her. She saw how his shoulders were bowed and how the jacket seemed to hang loosely on him as if he had aged suddenly. She heard him call for her several times but now Mrs Dhali was listening to the sound of the train getting louder. She could hear the children singing and her daughter whispering the sounds of the train stations. She could hear the excitement in their voices as the train came nearer and then she heard them screeching as the sound lifted them, whirling them higher and higher and this time she didn't listen to her silence. She jumped over it, leaving it far behind and caught the sounds of the train and the children shouting and her daughter whispering and held them in her hands, for ever.

The day before my eighteenth birthday, Mum made my birthday cake. It was a ring shape with pink icing, white star shapes, silver balls and white candles. She had spent three hours in total, making the cake. There had been a failed attempt; a scorched, dry sponge which was now frozen for a future trifle. She had brought in the completed masterpiece as I lolled on the sofa in the lounge, watching TV.

'Well... what do you think?' she had asked.

'I love it, Mum... thank you.'

On my birthday, I sat at the kitchen table whilst my father hovered at the sink. I was reading the instructions to the generic craft kit my aunt purchased for me every year. This time it was a card kit; you cut and stuck bits of paper and sequins into some equally generic card that simply read: *With Love.*

'Is that for your Mum?'

'It's for anybody.'

Dad looked at what I was doing with the interest he displayed in anything that involved construction, but clearly he'd seen the pink and the sequins and so he turned his attentions to the kettle.

'Can I have coffee, Dad?'

'I suppose so.'

The echoes of bubbling water drowned out the music playing on the kitchen radio and the forgettable pop song was finally extinguished. The kettle gave a final purr and a click. The DJ began talking at speed, splicing his sentences with guffaws and breathy disbelief. I made out something about house-hunters. A young couple; first time buyers perhaps. Viewing a house with an estate agent, opening the front door to find a hanging corpse waiting for them by the banisters. Then in the lounge, a woman, the wife, wheelchair-bound and now asphyxiated; a degenerating body but the clarity of mind to know what she wanted and that her husband would take care of everything. Imagine the faces of the young couple! A garbled phone number, a request for callers' thoughts on euthanasia and then a quick slide into the next pop tune.

I picked up the scissors and began cutting out flowers. Dad placed a cup of coffee a safe distance away from my jutting elbows. 'Did you hear that?' I asked.

'What? The thing on the radio? Yeah. Oh well...'

'But it's awful!'

'Why? They're only dead bodies. What I wanna know is, did the estate agent make the sale!' He eased himself into his usual place at the table and sipped his drink.

'Well, I think it's horrible. I don't get it... why put your house on the market and then decide to kill yourself? They could have at least had the decency to do it elsewhere.'

'Well, she was in a wheelchair. It might have been a sudden decision, pet, it must take a lot of balls to kill yourself. Or get someone else to do it for you.'

'I guess so.'

I began cutting out leaf shapes and the outline of a butterfly. Dad paused and sipped at his drink again. He suddenly leant back in his chair. He laid his hands flat on the table and inspected the length of his nails, the only feminine gesture I have ever seen my father do. 'I can understand it though'.

He paused. 'I'd end it all if I was in that situation.'

'Well that's the point, isn't it? Presumably she couldn't do it herself... that's why her husband had to do it.'

'Oh yeah... I think that's what happened. It's just that... well, I can understand, that's all.' He took another sip of his drink and then quickly opened the back door. 'It's warm in here, isn't it?'

I nodded and picked up the glue stick. I stuck pink card to cream paper. I added one flower and then another. Next door's dog started barking and cut off Sinatra in his prime.

'Bloody jazz!' said Dad.

I reached for my coffee and found it cold. I stood and went to the kettle to make a fresh one. Whilst the water boiled I looked out at the street. There! Keith and Mary going past. Keith pushing Mary and struggling with her wheelchair on the curb. Damn! I forgot to thank them for my birthday card, something Dad insisted on even more nowadays, although I'd had cards from them all my life, each birthday and all the small triumphs in between, and I hadn't always said thank you. I'll do it later.

I reached up on tiptoe to the cupboard for the coffee granules just as Dad began to speak. 'I don't want to end up in a wheelchair, unable to take care of myself. I don't want that. I'll blow my brains out first. Either that or you'll have to do it for me.'

I sank back on my heels and gripped the coffee jar. 'What are you talking about? I can't do that... even if I wanted to! It's against the law for starters.' I spooned the granules into my mug.

'I know. I'm just saying that... that's what I want. You were only a baby when your other grandma, my mother, died, but in the end she didn't recognise anyone and if I get to that stage I want to die...'

'But...'

'When I'm not me any more and I can't do the things I want to... I want out.'

'And what if you can't? What if you get like that woman on the radio?'

'I dunno. I'll find a way, I guess.'

I poured hot water on the granules.

'I'm just saying, that's all... You might as well know it's what I want.'

I added milk from the fridge and stirred three times clockwise and three times anti-clockwise. I threw the spoon in the sink. It landed with a dull thud on the dishcloth. I blinked, blinked harder and picked up my coffee. 'I know.' I said.

I turned to find him looking at me. I took a sip of my coffee whilst I leaned against the sink. The radio began playing more of the detested big band. Dad sipped his coffee too and reached out to close the back door now the room had cooled.

'Hey... don't worry about it, pet. I'm just making conversation, that's all!'

That evening after tea, Mum brought the cake into the kitchen and after the candles were lit and the lights had been turned off, they all sang Happy Birthday. Out of embarrassment mostly, I kept my eyes glued to the cake. The pink icing looked plastic in the candle light; the silver balls were sinking in its depths and it had dribbled onto the cake board. Invisible wax dripped onto the white star shapes, leaving a gelatinous blob that slowly lost its shine. I closed my eyes and blew out the candles, and in the few seconds before someone reached the light switch, there was dark.

Colin is asleep under our duvet, on his back, different sections of today's paper strewn around him. There's an article about faces in one of the sections with a picture of a criminal from Italy. The journalist says that you can tell a person is a criminal by what they look like. The picture is fuzzy but I can see it's a stocky man. His eyes really stand out. They're looking, really looking, pushing out like headlights through fog. For a minute I think they're looking at me, but he must have been looking at the photographer who works at the jail.

I compare Colin's face to the Mafia boss with the staring eyes, and make a checklist in my head. His eyes are a little too close together; I check a box in my head. His lips are slightly pouty too, another mental check. Before I have time to find a third, he's rubbing his eyes and stretching.

'Saw a woman last night.' He waits for me to react. I don't because I know he's smiling. 'Alright, she was ninety-four.' He yawns and sniggers. 'Crazy thing is, her neighbours called me out. She went round to theirs, next door but one. He's a teacher, she's a cellist.' I reach across and take his hand, but he takes another stretch instead. 'She got them out of bed at three-thirty in the morning. She's plucky to wake a sleeping teacher.' He gets out of bed and pulls on some boxers, then he goes to rummage through one of the last boxes and continues his story while stacking tatty medical journals along the floor near the bed.

'When I got there she seemed alright, a bit dazed, but up, you know.' He forgets that I didn't graduate sometimes, just goes straight into a case like I'll be able to diagnose from clues. 'So I asked her what hurts etc, the usual, and listened to her chest. Normal.' He flips through one of his old physiology books. 'What she said though,' he waves his hand. 'She was out of it. She was hearing voices. Nothing in my case could sort that out, maybe nothing on Earth could sort that out. I was stumped. Know where I'm going with this yet?'

'A head-case?' I ask, moving into the kitchen to fill the kettle.

'So I keep asking her questions and little by little it all comes out.' He slots the book carefully into place and stands up. 'She had one heck of a temperature.' He looks, sounds pleased with himself. 'So I gave her something to bring it down. After a while she started to relax and her talking got a little more sane. And before I know it, or the neighbours know it, I've figured it out. Bam! Just like that.' At this, he hurls an old ball of packing tape towards the kitchen bin through the ugly, veneered hatch that connects to the dining room. He misses and goes to retrieve it. His voice is hollow and high on the tiles. 'Urinary tract infection!'

'How was I supposed to get that?'

He hands me an empty mug and a coffee spoon. 'Clues were all there, babe. Learn from the master.' He gestures towards the percolator in the corner. I accept this defeat but refuse to make him proper coffee. Later, as I collect the newspaper up, I rip out the article about faces for my wall.

My client arrives at four. She says to call her Ella. I show her into the studio. The sky-light means that the illumination is perfect in there for painting. I adjust the easel as she looks around the walls. 'Don't you get distracted?' she asks, pointing a finger at the clippings and photographs littering the surfaces. She looks natural, like she's never wanted or needed makeup. Her grey hair is long and held with two red clips on the sides of her head. Her teeth are perfect; she must have had braces as a kid.

'I wouldn't make much money if I did.'

'Fair's fair. This you?' She's found a baby picture near the door. She looks back at me, smiling. 'Bet that's you. Don't you worry about getting paint on everything? You ever pick up a brush and go mad? I would. It'd be better than sex.' I take her word for it and pick up a pencil. 'Want me on this?' She perches on the stool near the only clear wall. It has years of dry paint stuck to it. I bought it just after I dropped out of medicine. 'I feel like I'm going to be shot, or something. You got a gun back there? Bet you have, just in case, you know. It's ok, I have one too.'

I look up from rummaging through a cluster of blank canvases near the bay window. She sees me look and smiles. 'Well for heavenssakes honey, I don't mean on me now, where would I stash a whopping great rifle?' She points to her torso. She's slim, but her jeans seem tighter than her skin.

'Point taken.' I continue looking for a canvas that will suit the price range we spoke about on the phone.

'Let's have that!' She leaves the stool and points to a large one I prepared last night. It's much more of a project than we discussed and almost twice the price. 'I don't care a hoot,' she exclaims. 'Get that bad boy up on the easel and let's see you throw some paint around.'

We settle it on the easel together and she sits back down. I pick up a newly-sharpened pencil. 'What are you going to use that for? Picking winkles?' I look back at her, confused. 'All you need is a big brush, honey, and a tub or your hottest pillar-box. And be quick about it, I've got a train at four.'

I'm in the kitchen carving up a butternut squash when I hear the door slam. It's getting dark earlier now so I can't paint as long. I call out to Colin, let him know where I am. He calls out too. Calls me sweetheart. 'Seen any more women?' I joke.

Losing his playful smile, he swings his medical case onto the hatch with a slam that startles me. Chunks of orange flesh litter the counter. 'What?' He looks straight at me.

'I said, seen any more women?' I continue to hack at the vegetable. 'You look wiped. Too many call-outs?'

He leans his hands onto the sides of the hatch and breathes out. He loosens his tie. 'Can you just stop beating up that lump of vegetable for two seconds?'

My knife hovers for a second and I put it down. 'Did you lose one?'

'A patient?'

'Yeah.'

'No.'

I walk round to his side of the hatch and put my hand under his jumper, letting my wedding-ring glide over his skin. He used to love it. 'Then... what?'

He takes my hand, squeezes it, and lets it fall. It has an orange hue to it, from the squash. As I look at the colour he walks away. The neatness he set out with has gone. He falls, rumpled, into a chair. I try for a bit longer but can't get anything out of him. I even try telling him about my day; how good, and red, it's been. I give up telling him how I was going to make him a wonderful meal. He becomes absorbed in something on the television and I fall asleep in our bed alone. The orange chunks of squash still lie on the sideboard, softening in the chilly darkness.

The high street is very crowded for a Thursday morning. Somebody selling something approaches me but I just move quickly on. I pick up Colin's suits from the dry cleaner's just as he asked. As I head back to the car I see a man drawing on the pavement. There's a stub of chalk in his gnarled hand. He makes jerky movements across the concrete, putting his whole body into it. He's on all fours, working with different colours. A family stop to watch next to me, and he works to the crowd. As he crawls back to collect more chalk from a folded pouch, I glimpse what he's sketching. It's nothing that I recognise but it seems like he's drawn it a thousand times. He puts lines in that don't make sense, like there's a template only he can see. A woman's face looks up from the cold stone. He uses the side of a peachy chalk stump to fill her broad lips in. Somehow he uses blue in her cheeks but she doesn't look sullen. He removes his coat and works faster, his beard stirring with every gesture. The lines are thickening and the woman becomes almost animated.

There's quite a crowd now, and someone has brought him a cup of tea. He gives the young girl a quick wink and returns his eyes to the ground. The drink turns cold as he takes more time over this woman's eyes. Clutching the chalk in different fingers, he uses the wrinkled index to blend the foggy colour down. I admire the sweeping motion of his hand, like he's shaping invisible pottery. Its curvature traces down and round with a loving slowness. He stands suddenly, and silently appraises his efforts. Strolling around his handiwork in contemplation, he seems contented with the image he has nurtured into shape. The crowd disperses and the old man replaces his materials in the folding pouch.

I meet Colin for lunch. He doesn't have long before afternoon surgery so we go to the hamburger bar around the corner. We order at the bar and take some seats near the big windows overlooking the car park. I ask him how his day's been. His face is lined. I hadn't noticed before, but the harsh strip lights really bring them out. He looks around him, and plays with his napkin until the food arrives. I try to tell him about the chalk man but he's more interested in his food. We eat our burgers in silence.

'Anna...' he begins, then stops, not looking at me.

'Colin...' I say, playfully. I touch my foot against his but he stays on his side of the booth, like he does on his side of the bed.

'I'm just going to tell you, because it's important that you know.'

I stop smiling at him and my feet swing under my chair. He tells me that he's been sleeping with a woman at work. He tells me that she's a doctor too and that it's been going on for a few weeks now. Somehow, I sit and listen to this terrible story, under the unforgiving tungsten glow. Stale chip grease hovers in the place, I feel like the shiny metal is closing in like a prison. I think of the eyes of the Italian mobster. Colin looks surprised when I get up and walk out.

The afternoon air is chilly but it's better than in there. Everyone on the street is doing what they need to do; they don't know what I know. They don't care. I don't realise what's happened until I've walked a couple of hundred metres down the road. I'm cold. It's only then I realise I forgot my coat, my bag. I forgot to say anything. As I walk home I try to think about what I need. By the time I get there, I've decided. Ella loves the idea of another sitting and comes straight to the house.

I'm already in the studio when she arrives. Her canvas has been drying in the corner of the room. I left the door on the latch for her and she finds me inspecting the painting. She says that there could be more red in it. 'It's about the white spaces as much as it is about the red marks,' I tell her. We look and nod at the canvas together as if we are learning about a piece in a gallery.

She claps her hands. 'Right, honey, let's get this fella done and dusted. I'm on my break at work; they think I'm in the staff lounge.' I don't laugh and she furrows her brow at me. 'You alright?' Her red hair clips have been replaced by green ones, like thin leaves poking out of her mass of grey. I put my brush bristles down into the jam jar. The water shifts and the red disperses, like a gnarled finger is blending it down. As I watch it swirl she comes down off the stool and over to me.

Before I know it, I've told her everything. How he ended our marriage over a burger. How he had been cold and I should have known. How he never liked my cooking. I laugh, she doesn't. Instead, she goes through to the kitchen and I hear her opening and closing cupboards. When she comes back she has a bottle of single malt whisky. Colin's. And two mugs, one from the Natural History museum and the other advertising Paracetamol. She takes the latter and we sit down next to the easel.

'Way I see it is... you're lucky.' The whisky is hard to take but I get the first glass down. She knocks it back with ease. 'Sounds like it was doomed from the start. He's given you an excuse to get the hell out.' I almost choke on my whisky. 'No, no, really. What does he do for you?' I cast an eye around the room, thinking. I realise that she is probably right. 'I'm right, aren't I?' She refills my glass. I realise that hardly any of the pictures on the wall are of Colin and me. I also realise that he hasn't come home to tell me that he actually loves me and it's all been a terrible mistake. This must show in my face. 'Don't start wanting him back.' She throws the rest of her whisky down her throat, looks me in the eyes, hard. It's like she's trying to see something through the fog. Although I'm not looking at her, I can see her.

'Wake up, honey, and have a hard think about what that son of a bitch did.' The words come out harshly in the silent room. We sit there for a moment, very close to the easel. I look up and can see the fibres in the canvas. I want to know why and how it happened.

'You want me to draw you a goddamn diagram?' Ella scowls. As I shake my head she looks down at the carpet. 'How attached are you to this rag?'

'Why?' I ask, bemused. We both study the thin textile.

'This must be the biggest picture we could have you paint right now.' She gets up and her eyes flick around the floor. Her eyes get wider as she walks around, occasionally stooping to feel the surface, like assessing a football pitch for play. 'It's perfect. Help me move this.' Getting up, I feel the alcohol is taking hold. We shift everything onto the bay window sill. She hands me the biggest brush and takes one for herself.

I apply the first mark. The red sits on the pleated twine for a moment and then seeps down. She swings her arm down and swipes the bristles against the surface. She dips the brush into the pot again and doesn't wipe it. A large splodge of blood-red hits the floor. She looks at me. I look at the brush in my hand. I wait for a second and then get to work.

We take turns to dip. I'm on my hands and knees, filling the space right over to the corners. She keeps the whisky coming and we're laughing now. In places, I stab the brush into the fibres of the carpet. Ella's eyes flash when she sees me do this. She does the same. We open another tin, this time pouring it straight onto the surface. It expands like lava. We're really tearing across the floor now; there's not much dirty beige left to cover. We keep right on going, through another tin. Soon, the light betrays us and we can barely make out our marks: hundreds of red, blazing, staring eyes.

At three-fifteen, Cliffside (conservative, Conservative, Christian) County Primary gets unlocked. It's three-twelve when I arrive at my fucked-up-fuck-up-single-father-widower-atheist-I-don't-fit-here-leave-me-the-fuck-alone-I'm-busy-being-lonely-feeling-shit-and-thinking spot at the back of the queue.

Then I leave my spot, walk the couple of metres to the edge, and look for the sea. But the tide's barely started coming in: water looks a long way off; can't hear it at all. Should I never have moved us? Restart. Kent coast. Two years ago it seemed a good thing. Maybe the wind will really blow big and take us somewhere else. I go back to my queue-coordinate.

Somebody sprayed orange, this term's PTFA Chair, I think, is huddle-talking. Undulating, high-pitch voice: 'I finally got a text this morning from B&Q. They look really good in the pink basket by the fire.' This updates me on a conversation broadcast earlier in the week about a wait on synthetic decorative logs to accessorise new living-flame hearth.

The huddle makes sing-song yes-noises. So much here gets said in that way. I think about the Bob Dylan line: *You know you always say that you agree*, and wonder if I should write it in wax crayon across the ground we queue on, like I used to do the alphabet for Emily along our garden path. Rains, hails, frosts, snows used to take an autumn and a winter to wash away the letters.

I'm just noticing that the huddles all seem to be dressed a bit like cowboys when I hear steps stop a few paces behind me. I turn round and see the mother new to the school queue. Her son's joined Edward VII (Year 3 class; Year 6 is Elizabeth II and they work it in reverse from there; they'll have to jiggle it all back one when Elizabitch quits or dies); the same class Emily's in. I've not seen this new person close up before; I take my chance now. Not only is she not painted orange, I can see her face 'cause she's make-up free. God (not that s/he exists): flesh; features! I could almost get the horn. Neither is she dressed like a cowboy. In fact she's in old-scruffy-stuff-doesn't-utterly-fit-charity-random (long green cardigan; man's white shirt; Los Angeles 1984 Olympics T-shirt; black cord skirt to wellington boots) which is no *look* at all. This isn't even studied chaos, student-chic or hippy. This is clothes-by-probability-no-clothes-really-at-all *her*. I can see a person.

We're less than a fortnight into the new school year but I'm saying she's already had enough and has fled the chirruping. I remember how to smile, and go over. 'What d'you think of it so far?' I mock-whisper.

She takes a second to look at me (sees green eyes, mess, jeans, the earth on my working-boots?) smiles back, then whisper-mouths, 'Bollocks.'

For Cliffside this is swearing! This woman uses language: I could weep and kiss the tarmacadam, but I just laugh. 'I'm Noah,' I say, holding out a hand. Now *she* laughs. 'I know,' I say. I'm thinking my name; I'm no Noah. Noahs aren't skinny-tall, gorse-headed (confused, and bushy-blond) Scotsmen that escape their Highland puritan kin only to roustabout, impregnate bad-idea junkie women, and forevermore fuck up.

'I'm not sure you do,' she says, still laughing.

'You're probably right,' I say, laughing too.

'Well it's just that I'm... I'm called Nelly,' she says, and shakes my hand (soft, eel electricity) and we both pause laughing.

'Like the TV show?' I say. 'When we were kids.'

'Yes, like the TV show.' Her accent sounds from Cornwall; she has these blue, sparkly, deep eyes, like the sea there.

'Well,' I say.

'Well,' she says. Jesus (real, but good at magic?): she is... *herself*... and that's... *fathoms*, and *beautiful*.

The queue moves. Me and Nelly walk in to fetch our children.

Ten-forty next morning is Harvest Festival Assembly. I wave hi to Emily, then notice Nelly's arrived ahead of me. She's standing at the back of the little hall. That's what I normally do too; you get a better view that way. Most of the rest of the parents are sat on the rows of plastic diddy-seats provided. Nelly waves, so I go across. 'Some spread,' she whisper-laughs, nodding at the table in the corner.

There's a tiny shy of canned goods (could knock it over from here; good aim on me), a packet of Waitrose Cornflakes, and a dented tin of Bird's Custard Powder: most people send their kids in with a quid (all monies and swill to W.I. for in-parish distribution). Behind the plastic fruit and veg the school puts out, though, I can see Emily's contribution. Carrots (eelwormed, but organic isn't easy) she pulled this morning, still earthy and with leaves; and some Wiljas (already many-eyed, but that's just potatoes saying hello) we pantried after August dig-out. Then I see something new, tucked away at the back, almost hidden by the dried custard and tinned-shit shy. On top of a picture of a Trident sub surfacing in the Clyde (the front page of Wednesday's, yesterday's, *Guardian*) is a real, shiny, sparkly, scaly, gills-fins-head-tail fish!

'The fish,' I say. 'That's... it's... fantastic. From Russ and you?' When we said goodbye, see you tomorrow, on the cliff-top after pick-up yesterday, Nelly explained that Russ and her live on a fishing-ketch sailboat. They've got a mooring in the harbour and she and Russ walked down the hill to there, while Emily and me walked along the cliff-top to our 'croft'.

'A sea-bass. Headmistress was not amused: "It'll *smell*. Go *off*." So I told her I didn't want to disappoint Russ after he'd hooked it himself last night, and that I'd be very happy to make salt-fillets later today, if needed. Is that fresh veg, putting soil all over her lovely school, from that very-southern-croft of yours then?'

'I confess.'

'Vegetable-criminal,' she says, and makes as if to tweak me in the ribs.

'Fish-vandal,' I say, and smile, and look at her again, and notice how now her hair's down (yesterday it was pinned); just how long it actually is (all the way over the crests of her breasts to the crests of her bum); and as rich and as black as the Quink I used to fill my fountain pen with when I was a pupil at primary school.

Then, Headmistress on synthesizer. 'All Things Bright and Beautiful' starts up (instrumental version: Deputy-Headmistress holds up a sign that says *Do Not Sing Yet!*) and vicar enters. Vicar (new, looks about seventeen) has a cloak on (like some sort of fucking Wild West sheriff). Once he reaches microphone-on-a-stand (PTFA's latest purchase) stage-front-centre, Headmistress cuts the music. Then (what-the-fuck?!) he microphones-out the starts of sentences that the kids finish by reading the series of signs that Deputy-H holds up.

'God's light is called the...'

'Sunshine!'

'God's water is called the...'

'Raintime!'

'God's beds are called the...'

'Soil fine!'

'God gives us lots of...'

'Good time!'

'And these together bring...'

'Harvest Festival!'

'Except that bit didn't...'

'Quite rhyme!'

'This is insane,' Nelly says.

'I know it,' I say.

'Aw! Sweet!' the parents say, and I see that most have either camcorders or mobile phones aloft.

'Is it always...' Nelly says.

'It's getting worse,' I say.

The Vicar does an I'm-lifting-my-hands-up-so-you-all-get-to-your-feet gesture and the kids stand. Then he sort of sways on the spot as if in rapture and re-microphones each of the identified God-gifts but this time with accompanying actions which the kids have to copy.

'Sunshine!' is wiggling fingers from above head down to ground.

'Raintime!' is much the same, but somehow you know it's rain, and there's a Mexican Wave as well.

'It's like some sort of Nazi rally,' Nelly says.

'Maybe we should Tin Drum it,' I say.

'Soil fine!' is smoothing hands at ankle-level.

'Good time!' is tapping imaginary watches (the kids aren't allowed to wear them because of health-and-safety) and then making your right arm tick seconds like it's on a clock.

'Harvest Festival!' closes it with each of the actions once more until a finale of stimulated clapping and cheering.

Headmistress, Cheshire-catting, starts again on 'All Things Bright and Beautiful' (up-tempo version with pronounced-strings-effect) and Deputy-H holds up a sign that says *Sing Now!*

'What did you mean, Tin Drum it?' Nelly says.

Maybe it's just male showing-off, but I say, 'I'll show you,' and I walk to the front.

Just behind Harvest Festival Table is the piano the synthesizer demoted. I squeeze round to it and lift the lid. I put my foot down on the echo-pedal and play loud. John Lennon's 'Imagine'. Just as the hall is reaching 'The purple-headed mountains, the river running by,' I'm at my opening vocals, bellowing: 'Imagine there's no Heaven, it's easy if you try.' Nelly's stood beside me in time to join in with 'No hell below us, above us only sky.' Her voice is deep and loud and rich. I can hear laughter, chaos, crying and booing, and the Headmistress playing louder to compete, even though nobody's singing her song anymore. Nelly and I are relishing 'Imagine all the people living life in peace' when Deputy-H tries to slam the lid down. But Nelly's there first and holds it in place. This brings Cook out who bundles the Wiljas, carrots, and sea-bass into her apron and drops them out onto the keys. I keep playing and singing anyway (Nelly too) until we get to deliver: 'You may say I'm a dreamer, but I'm not the only one, wuh-hoo-hoo-hoo-hoo' when I stand, take Nelly's hand in mine (soft-spark-eel-feeling again), and lead us in a bow. I see all the kids are being ushered out of the hall but I manage to wave hi to Emily again who looks happy enough. In fact, she gives me a smile and a thumbs-up. She's walking with Russ and he looks fine too. Kids are very adaptable.

Me and Nelly are in H's office, with H, Deputy-H and Agent-Orange-Cowboy (she *is* this term's PTFA Chair). There are bars on the window. They are all sat on swivel-seats behind a giant-slab-of-glass-on-metal desk. We are on plastic diddy-chairs on the floor-space. 'Well?' H says.

We say nothing.

'Headteacher has asked you a question,' Deputy says.

'Did she?' I say.

'Leave the talking to me please, Sandra,' H says.

Deputy scowls at us.

'Perhaps, Miss Evetide, being new to Cliffside, you might make it a priority to keep *good* company and set *good* examples for Russell, who, as I understand it, we took on here in good faith despite your unconventional lifestyle, nomadic history and his lack of in-school schooling.'

'My son's name is Russ,' Nelly says. 'And boats, moving about, bisexuality and sperm donation have brought a lot of joy.'

Three wide mouths. Nelly, you're amazing.

H de-stuns herself. 'Moving on. I did not see you, Mr Adamson, as so *proactive* a revolutionary.'

I laugh. 'Maybe not.'

'I know a good doctor,' she adds.

'I bet you do,' I say.

Nelly laughs. H tuts.

'Is it that you are a bad influence on each other?'

We don't reply.

'Right. An emergency meeting of the Governors will be called. Pending that I impose upon you both an emergency-powers suspension from all assemblies, productions, fundraisers and concerts.'

'Any of those forthcoming?' I ask.

'That is not your concern. PTFA Outreach may contact either or both of you, should they so decide. Good morning.'

Once we're off the premises (Caretaker escorts) Nelly can't stop laughing. This sets me off. We walk, laugh, snort, giggle. On the cliff-top, where the path to the harbour and the path to my croft meet, we pause. 'I've got to do a bit of caulking on the boat while the tide's still out,' she says. 'But I'll see you at pick-up?'

'Yes. See you then, Nelly. And thanks.'

'No. Thank you,' she says. The wind is coming in gusts off the sea. Her hair is being lifted and billowed; I think of waves coming in at night.

'What's caulking?' I ask.

'It's sealing up the boat's wood, with hot tar. Getting it really ready again. What are you going to do?'

'Um. Think. And till. The usual.'

Nelly laughs. 'Right.'

'Right,' I say.

Then we take our paths home.

By the time I turn the corner and see the pick-up queue it's three-ten. Nelly's already there, stood apart from the cowboys. Seeing her with her black hair in a long plait gives me an idea about noising-up these cowboys a bit, but I decide I won't suggest it to her yet. 'Hi,' I say.

'Hi,' she says.

We're about six feet away from the last huddle. They're chirruping, but very quietly. Whole words can't be heard, just muffled snips and squeaks. They're in tactile-overdrive. Nelly and me, stood here, are the must-be-ignored, but our activities are the obvious-new-sensation. The queue-people remind me of wind-up toys. I got a wind-up cowboy one

Christmas when I was about Emily's age. I think it went rusty when I left it out in the rain.

'You okay, Nelly?'

'I'm good. You?'

'Good too. How was the hot tar thing?'

'Smelly. But I got it done in time. Before the tide came in again.'

Then we see H and Deputy-H coming to the gate with Emily and Russ. The other children must still be in their classrooms. H unlocks the gate, sends Emily and Russ out, then relocks it. Headbitchress and Deputy-Headbitchress stand there watching whilst the huddles silence themselves and we walk forward to meet the children, and Emily joins hands with Russ and they walk to meet us. The huddles make way for both us and the kids. Then Nelly takes my hand (more soft, eel electricity; even in these circumstances) and we've reached the children. Emily comes to take my other hand, and Russ takes Nelly's, and we walk back the four of us in a line, the huddles having to move even further apart to let us through. While we're walking through the parted cowboys, Russ says, 'Kids have been teasing us about what you and Emily's Dad did, Mum.'

'What did you say to them, sweetheart?' she says.

'I told them to fuck off, Mum.'

'Good lad,' she says.

Muted gasp from huddle; Agent Orange agape as the Dartford Tunnel.

'Are you okay, Emily?' I say.

'I'm fine,' she says. 'I kicked a boy.'

'Did you?' I say, managing not to laugh.

'But he's had it coming for a long time. He's a Year 6 table-leader and he forces the infants to eat stuff they don't like. He called Russ weird, then he called me ugly, then he said you and Nelly were weird and ugly, so I kicked him. And told him to get fucked too.'

'I think you did what you had to do, darling,' I say.

We pass through the final dispersed huddle and keep walking. Hyper-chirruping recommences once we've carried on a few steps and they've seen we're only heading home.

At the place where the harbour path and the croft path meet, we halt. Because of the way the land lies the sea looks a long way off, but it's really just below us, and I can hear it rushing over the rocks even though it looks quite calm in the distance. Nelly is checking something with Russ. My mobile beeps. I go to inbox and the display says Cliffside School. I press for the message: *NO school tmw for emily, 1 day suspension for bullying and language. letter to follow. Headteacher and Team.*

Then Nelly's mobile beeps. She reads her message and laughs. 'What are you doing tomorrow?' she says.

'Probably the same as you,' I say.

'Thought so,' she says. 'How about a jaunt on the boat then, the tar will have set and have stopped being so smelly by then.'

'Emily,' I say. 'D'you fancy that?'

'Don't I have to go to school?'

'Not tomorrow,' I say.

'Great,' she says.

'Can I stay home too, Mum?' Russ says.

'Of course,' Nelly says.

'Looking forward to it then,' I say. 'Thanks.' I think we're about to say 'right' or 'well', probably say a time for tomorrow, before parting ways, when I surprise myself. 'Nelly,' I say. 'Would you and Russ like to come back for tea? I've got this idea I'd like to run by you all.'

'Russ?' she says.

'Great,' he says.

'I can show you round the croft, Russ,' Emily says.

'Thanks, Noah,' Nelly says, 'I'd like to see where you've been living, sample some of those vegetables, and wait until the boat's good and ready.'

Emily and Russ are sleeping. A cliff-top of fresh air, some game-and-veggie hotpot, and another run round the croft when Harris showed up (he's a three-legged fox we found on the roadside not long after we moved here who still stops by for hellos and handouts) and they flaked. They look so deep-asleep and at ease that I wonder if they're hibernating. We tuck a blanket around them (they're on the big couch in the kitchen) and me and Nelly go through to the lounge and sit on the sofa. 'You haven't said your idea yet,' she says.

'It's still sort of taking shape,' I say. 'But it came to me when I saw you with your hair plaited.'

'Do tell,' she says.

'Have you noticed they're dressed like cowboys; the queue-people? This season's *look* I suppose.'

'Yeah, I have,' she says, and laughs.

'Well, I wondered if we might carry on our protest. I don't think I can bring myself to ask Emily to tolerate Cliffside anymore anyway, so I thought it would be good to go out with principles held aloft and fast. I'm thinking a protest-camp, with a teepee and us decked-out in indigenous clobber. Offer the queue-cowboys an alternative vision.'

Nelly laughs. She looks beautiful: happy. 'Noah,' she says. 'I love the idea. I think we should work on it as soon as we get back from our sail.'

'Great,' I say.

Then she moves up the sofa so she's right next to me; whoa and wow and Jesus: her being so close is more of that eel-electricity; all of a sudden, all at once, and all down the length of where she is; down the whole side of my body. She takes my face into her hands (an eel inside my head) and brings it gently close to hers, where she holds it so we're kiss-close and looking at each other. There are eels swimming in her eyes; I want to dive in; I kiss her.

God. I stop kissing her almost at once. This is melting.

'It's okay,' she says. 'It'll be okay.'

'I don't know what this is,' I say.

'Me either. But I think it's just two people finding each other, Noah. Being human.'

I kiss her again. This time it's eel-rain in my head. I'm... very, very glad. 'Nelly, you're not some sort of... it's not like in that Wim Wenders film where there's angels on the Underground, is it?'

She laughs, takes my hand, and slides it down the front of her skirt, all the way to where she's waiting. It's wet-fire. Man, she's an oven, a furnace, a bonfire-in-a-waterfall. 'I'm just a woman, Noah,' she says, 'and a very horny, once lonely one, if you want to know.'

'I do,' I say.

God, she... her... feels *so*...

'Can you imagine how good it'll...' I say.

'Yes,' she says.

So we do. And it's tropical-forest-rainstorm-with-lightning; it's the ocean and rivers, full of eels and tiny little electric fish, where the ocean and rivers are both water and fire. Somewhere in me (right in my reaches, in my deepest, furthest pockets) and elsewhere, out far away in the world, something shifts and happens. A glacier goes quick not slow maybe; a volcano surges and blows; a wind picks up big on the water.

God, am I getting carried away? I know I do that. But in a minute we'll sleep so we're good for the morning. We'll fall into sleep to the sound of the rain at the roof, the window, the chimney; because that's the rain on now.

The town was hot and swollen gold in the midday sun and Susan was sitting in the dirt. She found that if she sat still for long enough and positioned her legs in the correct way, strange insects would wriggle out from beneath the sand and grit and slowly and methodically march up her shins. They had hard, blue backs and tiny pinchers that nicked her skin. When they reached the smooth undulation of her knees she flicked them away with rigid fingers and they fell back into the sand, sometimes on their backs, legs flailing. They would re-bury themselves under the dark sand or take another chance on the craggy pass that was her limbs. Her mother once said they would bite her and she would fall ill, and then she'd regret sitting out on a Libyan street like some uneducated urchin. Susan's younger sister had crinkled her nose at that idea. She thought her sister uncouth, and she was only four.

Susan watched her insects congregate for a while longer before she grew bored and left them with an airy sigh. She was only allowed down to the bottom of the street, so she wandered over there, just to test her mother's limits, and leant against a wall that was clinging onto a small shard of shade. All of the buildings on the street were straight and grey. None of them leaned and none of them were painted. They all stretched up unerringly towards the fierce blue sky, windows opening up against the blank walls like black, sullen pockmarks. Out of these windows spewed limp washing lines upon which hung discoloured robes and sheets that fluttered and waved in the rare breeze. When they moved they made noises that were stiff and puckering.

You could always tell which of the soldiers were American and British by the way that they smoked. Laconic, at ease with themselves and the world, they would let the cigarette hang from their bored lips or hold it in an outstretched or limp hand, brushing against their thighs. The smoke would curl up and rest over their heads, making the hot day even hotter, and when they had finished they would flick the crumpled and charred stub into the sand with a deft flick of the hand. Sometimes, if the stub was unfinished, someone would creep over; a local, bent with embarrassment, would fish it out from the sand and take deep, theatrical drags on the spent tobacco, always grinning. The soldiers didn't seem to notice and would carry on walking while this local, dressed in white cotton robes, would gorge himself on their throwaways. Susan thought this certain one lived on the dilapidated street next to hers and she watched him with distaste until he looked up and winked at her and she had to turn away because her mouth was bulging with a barely-suppressed grin.

The soldiers recognised her up against the wall and came over, all smoking and all covering their eyes from the glare that the street kicked up. 'That's Robert's daughter, right?' one of them said, and there was a murmuring of agreement and they all took a drag on their cigarettes and looked about the street.

Susan recognised one of the men as someone who had once come to her house for supper. He was small and round with nervous hands and an awkward smile. They'd had soup and his table manners had been so unassumingly awful that Susan had had to force spoonfuls of the steaming, salted broth into her mouth to stop from laughing. He belched at the end of the meal and noticed Susan squeak with hysteria, and for the rest of the evening he stayed quiet, abashed and ever so polite. He was Irish, and Susan found him endearing, like a puppy that wasn't yet housetrained.

'How's your Dad?' they asked.

Susan shrugged. She hadn't seen him for a few weeks now. The last time he'd come home they'd gone to the beach for the day. It had been windy and the ocean had rolled against the sea wall in huge, creamy curls. Her father's face was burnt a deep brick red and he had smoked and shielded his eyes from the sun and in the late afternoon he'd waded into the sea with Susan and taught her the breaststroke. She told the soldiers this and they nodded in a disinterested way.

Her mother appeared from down the street. She was wearing an apron and her face was flushed red from cooking and the soldiers greeted her and they talked about things that Susan couldn't really understand. A large portion of each day in Benghazi was consumed by the unknown: strange words, places, people and rituals. Susan had come to be unfazed by it. The whole reason why they were there was an unknown, but she remembered the day her parents told her that they were leaving England. They had shown her pictures of this golden land that seemed to be a well of heat and spices and for a moment she was frightened. She crawled into bed, clutching her teddy, holding it against her chest, thinking about the playground she went to every Tuesday with its aluminium slide and cold, hard climbing frame, and how her mother told her she would have to be grown up and brave and think of this as an adventure, and then she said the name of the town, Benghazi, out loud, addressing her room and her belongings. 'Benghazi!' she said, almost coyly at first. The room didn't seem too bothered. She said it again, making her voice sound excited, then sad, and then angry. She rolled the name about on her tongue, separated it into chunks, put an emphasis on certain parts – 'Ben-gha-ZI!'. She grew excited and kicked back the covers of her bed and danced about her room in her nightclothes. Benghazi. Benghazi. Benghazi. Her nine-year-old heart seemed to be pumping along to the beat of the syllables. 'BENGHAZI!' She shrieked at her toys. She opened her wardrobe and bellowed at her clothes, 'BENGHAZI!' She pulled back her curtains and looked out at her small, grey garden and whispered, deliciously, *Benghazi*.

Susan's mother persuaded the soldiers to take Susan to the market with them. Unerringly polite, they wouldn't dream of refusing, but Susan could see from the way they shuffled their feet against the ground that they would be embarrassed to have an eleven-year-old girl trailing along behind them, skipping over their discarded cigarette buts. The belching Irishman was ordered to take care of her, and Susan fancied that she could see the memory of their supper together dancing in his eyes, as when she took his hand he flinched but didn't let go. Too polite to even refuse a little girl, Susan mused. His hand was sweaty and whole around hers, like a mollusc, with her small, pink fingers protruding like tiny sea-urchins. They set off towards the market. The cigarette smoke stung her eyes more than the sun.

People snatched at things in the market. Bearded men snatched money from the fists of their customers, pick-pockets snatched peoples' wallets from their loose bags while Susan watched, bemused. People even snatched at Susan herself. Women in burqas, settled in the shade, pinched at her pink arms, fascinated by her browning, freckled skin, and babbled unknown compliments. They tried to get her to stop and look at their stalls: rickety tables riddled with woodworm but covered with beautiful and ornate necklaces, brooches, rings, earrings.

'Stolen, no doubt,' Susan's Irish carer muttered to himself as he handed over a couple of notes to buy a brooch for Susan, to stop the women from grabbing at her. The women waved as Susan was hoisted up onto Irish's shoulders, away from the scrum. She waved back, and when they were a safe distance away she opened her cupped fists and saw an opal set in rusted gold. The stone was smooth and cool and covered with milky streaks of blue and green, like the sea on a stormy morning.

The American soldiers liked to stop and talk to any women not wearing long, heavy burqas. From her vantage point on the soldier's shoulders, Susan delicately assumed it was some sort of cultural question that they asked these women. They never seemed to mind. Lingering in the shadows thrown by the market stalls they were, to Susan, all powdered flesh; their deep and luscious skin toned down to a pale sickly colour by cheap makeup, the waistbands of their skirts too tight and constricting so that the skin on their stomachs became puckered and dented. They scraped long, blood-red nails along the arms of one soldier, intoning appreciatively in a nasal Arab voice, while he looked bemused, excited and enamoured all at once. The soldiers guffawed and Susan pressed her face against Irish's and asked if those women were his friends. He wriggled with embarrassment and quickly took Susan from his shoulders and pushed her imploringly into the crowd. 'Go and have fun!' he hissed urgently before turning back to the matter at hand.

Susan got lost very quickly. She wandered listlessly, pinching at the skin on her arms and freckled chest and remembered an incident back in England. Her mother had dressed up to go out to dinner one evening and she had come into the kitchen, unforgiving heels clacking against the cool, tiled floor. Susan's father had suddenly appeared, as if materialising out of the darkness, and with large hands he had grabbed at the flesh on Susan's mother's hips, pressed his lips to her ear and whispered, '*Mine*.' Susan and her sister, watching from the dinner table, had grinned at each other and covered the smirks from their parents with chubby fists. But there was something about the look on her father's face, and how this look slipped awkwardly onto her mother's, that gradually stopped Susan from laughing. She stopped laughing and stopped smiling and just watched her father's hands on her mother's hips, tight, and all-consuming, and her mother's expression, laughing, but behind this, a certain tenseness. And Susan realised, gradually, as she moved through the huge, murmuring mass of the market that this tenseness, like a sharp intake of breath, or the nervous clenching of a hard-set jaw, was lingering, just as it had with her mother, behind the expressions of the soldiers' 'friends', and in the intensity of the covered-women's snatching hands.

Later that evening, Susan lay on her bed, stripped down to her underpants because of the suffocatingly heavy heat. She clutched at her empty stomach which had rolled and rumbled since she'd been sent to bed without any dinner. The soldiers had traipsed along to the house twenty minutes after Susan had returned. The task of explaining that they'd lost her had been passed onto Irish, who, lost completely in his emotional speech, had trundled on for at least three minutes before he had noticed Susan standing behind her mother, a scowl on her face. Irish was sweating profusely, his flabby pink hands nervously fiddling with his pockets under Susan's hard gaze. He mentioned nothing of the painted women, only how Susan had wriggled artfully from his grip and the last he had seen of her was the lace trim of her summer dress slipping through the packed crowds. Susan stared, outraged and betrayed, as her mother apologised and offered them dinner. They declined with great dignity and as they moved off down the street an American said in an overly loud voice, 'and I thought she was such a good kid!' and they laughed belligerently. Susan's hands had trembled with indignity. And Susan's mother's response to her daughter's story of the women lingering hopefully in the shade? 'We don't speak about things like that.'

Susan was sure she had witnessed the forbidden, or at least some small piece of her possible future. Not necessarily decked out in rusted jewellery and tight, clamping clothes, or even long, all-consuming robes, but forever in the shade, lingering eternally in the shade, with hands outstretched, beseeching, calling on the blazing men that pass; calling constantly for some compassion.

Susan lies in her bed and when the insects and flies land deftly on her legs she can tolerate them no longer and shifts, so that they lift up and spiral lazily through the air. Outside, in the backyard, as always, chickens are being slaughtered for the next day's market. Their terrified clucks and cries drift softly across the night and Susan is so accustomed to the sight that she doesn't even have to watch; she can re-create the images behind closed eyes. There is the blade shining in the moonlight, and a smooth rush of air as it carries itself down and through the struggling chicken's neck. For a moment everything is still, and then, every once in a while, the chicken will leap to its feet, delirious with confusion, and strut and race, unseeing, across the dirt while its head lies on the ground next to a man's sandal-clad feet. Susan remembers watching from her bedroom window one night as a beautiful chicken, with sleek, dark feathers, ran and ran for hours with no head, only a bloodied, bulbous stump where it used to be and desperation and hope running through its veins. Some never regain motion, some stumble and fall after seconds, but this one chicken kept moving, gliding over the grit, its flapping wings dark smudges against the walls. And Susan cannot help but think how this act is recreated every day at the market. How the women strut and cower, covered or bare, yet always headless, and yet with the perception of remaining intact, and all the while with the men watching, leaning back on sandaled feet, and owning some part of the women, some part that is always kept in the shade.

The chickens' cries gradually die out, replaced by the soft honking of trains in the distance. Susan is holding the brooch from the market in her hand. The stone is cool and smooth and she presses it against her burning forehead, and then her freckled chest and then leaves it lying on her stomach. She finds that it fits perfectly in the cascading dip of her belly, and the green and blue of the streaked stone is vibrant against her lightly tanned skin. She thinks that she looks like some exotic princess. She drums her fingers against her hipbone and then, after a small hesitation, grips at the flesh there and boldly tells her bedroom, in a hushed, yet strong voice, 'Mine.'

_THE FOX

I don't know why I'm digging this hole. Shovel in, foot in, toss. We work apart in the heat of the yard. Doing our jobs. Boss says it's better that way. Shovel in, foot in, toss. 'Less fucking about yappin',' was what he said. Looking up, I see Albert stacking bricks on the scaffold and White Trainers clearing some broken slabs into the skip. White Trainers gives me a silent nod. I give a wave back. Shovel in, foot in, toss. Grip the handle. Shovel in, foot in, toss. The sun beats down on our dirty heads. A buzz bangs inside my head and my work shirt is salty sweat circles. Shovel in, foot in, toss. Stab, stab, stab. It's something hard. Scrape, stab, scrape the dirt away with the shovel.

It's a big old bent concrete slab. I jam the shovel head under the concrete slab and lever down. I push down but it doesn't move. Harder, harder and harder pressing the handle down, a salty sweat slipping down my nose into my mouth. I spit into the dry ground. Pressing down again and the handle snaps off, cutting my wrist. A red sliver slips in between the dirt on my forearm. I press my palm into the skin. Blood seeps out the sides and drips red onto the slab. Something falls on my head. I snap my head left... right. A cackle comes from above.

'Fucking hell, mate. Stop crying and put your cock into it. That slab ain't gonna lift itself.'

Albert. He's above my head and dangling his boots over the scaffold boards. I look up and see his crooked chimney teeth cackling down at me. He kicks another stone onto my head and shuffles his tired limbs away. I pick the handle up and smack it back on with the heel of my hand. I rub the dirt into the cut to slow the bleeding down. I slide the shovel under the slab again and push my weight down. I push hard, imagining when I push into Sarah; sliding in and out, her chin pointed up, face hidden. I push hard on the metal handle. It lowers enough for me to get my foot on it. I stamp down sharp. The slab coughs up, splattering earth, pebble, dirt and insect up into my face. I spit the earthy muck back into the hole left by the slab. A fat worm coils around in the mud. Hammers smack, drills blaze and mixers churn. The worm is pink and silent. Its body is struggling to find a way back into the ground.

'Tea time, mate. Do you want anything from the shop?' The voice comes from behind. The body slips into the muck. 'Fags? Sandwich? I think I owe you some money from the week before.'

'Go on then,' I say. 'Could you get us a 20 pack of Sovereign and a Mars?'

'Alright, yeah. No worries.'

I watch him drift off. White Trainers. I don't know his name. I never asked, he never told. He wears these shiny white Nike trainers, slashed with a big red tick. They're always fucked up by the end of the day, covered in muck. He comes in the next day and they're clean. I watch his whites curl around the gate down the road to the shop.

My back's against the blue metal container. I'm drawing out the last of the cigarette and fingering my cut. The site is quiet apart from the brickies who work through breaks. I start to listen to Albert and White Trainers. They're slurping on tea, Albert smoking a roll-up, White Trainers turning the paper. I turn and watch.

'Whatcha get up to on the weekend, son?' Albert asks.

'Not much. Went down Gazelle's. Roll us one of them,' White Trainers says, nodding at Albert's fag.

'Right oh,' says Albert. 'Yeah, I've heard of it. A club, init?' He spreads the tobacco on the Rizla.

'Yeah, it's a club.' White Trainers rolls his eyes towards me from behind his paper. I smile at him, pull myself up and sit on the bench next to Albert. He passes me the roll-up and I pass it to White Trainers.

'Never been there myself. Bet there's a lotta tits in there though. Get anything?'

'What?' White Trainers says.

'You know? Get your balls wet.'

'Nah. Nothing. Mostly guys getting...' White Trainers stops to light the roll-up. A few strands of tobacco stick out of the end. 'Pissed.'

'Bit shit then. Me. Old man bloke me. I was at Church all Sunday.'

'Hmm?' White Trainers says.

Albert cackles. 'Only the Church of the bloody Coach and Horses.' He bangs the side of the container and the sound echoes around the dust of the empty site. 'That's me, son. I'm always worshipping there. The only way I know how.' The room goes quiet. I tap the table, White Trainers smokes, grey wisps coming from behind the paper. Albert's looking at the front page, scratching his neck. 'Bombs in London, eh? Crazy fucking nutters. Lucky I don't have any family to lose, eh? Fuck me. I'm a funny cunt sometimes. Still, them boys must have some... you know?'

'What?' White Trainers says, leaning his head into the paper.

'Point. You know? A point. Sharp thing.' Albert makes a stabbing motion at me with the teaspoon. 'If you're gonna stab someone you've gotta have a point. No one does anything without having a point.'

'What are you on about, you stupid old cunt?' White Trainers says, lowering his paper, rolling his eyes at me.

'You won't understand. You're young; everything's booze, birds and fights to you. It's all yesterday, today, tomorrow. When you get a bit older, bit more experienced and that, you'll find out. We all do. You understand, don't you, boy?' Albert says, patting my arm with the back of his hand.

'Yeah,' I say quickly, rolling my wedding ring around with my thumb, under the table.

'The great philosophising labourer,' says White Trainers, getting to his knees in front of Albert. 'By day he shovels shit, by night he preaches to the millions. We truly are not worthy.'

'Get up, you prick. Do you know what I like about you?' Albert says.

White Trainers raises his head. 'What's that then, Mystic Meg?'

'Nothing,' Albert cackles, slapping his thigh. White Trainers smiles. I get up, stretch my back and wander to the Portaloo. It's hot and stinks of piss that's been left to thicken. The flush has stuck and no one has got round to fixing it. We're supposed to pour a bucket of water down instead, but no one does. I piss, shake off and step out, giving my hands a quick dunk in the cold water bucket outside. I look back to my hole. It doesn't look like I've done much.

The Boss's tin can canteen is on top of ours. He doesn't ever come out. I climb the staircase up to his door. My steps are heavy in my steel-capped boots. I knock on the door. No answer. So I knock again. The voice of my Boss comes through the steel. 'Yes? What is it?'

'Well... it's just... I was wondering... if you wanted me to keep doing this hole.'

'Did I tell you to stop?'

'No.'

'Then don't.'

Shovel in, foot in, toss. I stab my shovel in again and again. Flash and a rumble; thunder and lightning. Rain spits down on my head, wetting my hair and the shovel. I can feel my skin cooling in the patter. A drop drips in between my sock and skin. The fat drops colour blobs of the soil dark brown. I stab my shovel into the ground. It's softer and opens up. A splatter of the dirt licks my jeans. Shovel in, foot in, toss. Snap. I stop. Get down on my knees. My fingers dig into the ground. Feeling softness. Roundness? No, thin, hard? Hairy? My hand grips and pulls it out of the sludge. Push my legs and stand up. Holding it up in the air, rain slip-sliding the dirt off the fur.

A dead fox in my hands.

The smell fists into my nostrils. A black, dead smell; bitter and sharp. It's been dead for a while. What's left of the head and tail bent to the ground. Mangled face, eyes ripped and red. The mouth hanging open, the tongue shrivelled. The belly is open and lumpy guts hang down swaying in the wind. Looking down at it, I look down at me. Stomach, dick, legs, booted feet. I throw the dead fox back in the hole. Its mud dead face looks up at mine.

'What's that?'

'It's nothing. A dead fox,' I say. My leg goes back down.

'Is it?' asks White Trainers. 'What are you gonna do with it? Don't go touching it. They're fucking filthy animals. Carry all kinds of diseases. More than rats.'

'Really? I don't know, probably just throw it in the skip.'

'Fair enough. It's only a fox anyway, you know what I mean?'

'Yeah,' I say.

'Just get rid of it, alright, pal? I'm going back inside.' White Trainers turns back, dirt clinging to his trainers with every step.

Work's over. I key the door, it unlocks and I step inside. The heating is on and I can smell roasting meat. Computer game noises beep and jangle in the front room. I go in and Harry's sitting cross-legged. The controller is in his hand and he's staring at colourful things jumping about on the screen. He doesn't turn his head.

'Alright?' I say.

'Alright,' he says, not taking his attention off the screen.

'How was school?'

'Boring.'

'Yeah. That's how I remember it.' I go in and sit cross-legged beside him, our knees touching. 'Don't let your Mum hear that I said that though.' His fingers bash the buttons in frantic little patterns. 'You're good at this,' I say, pointing at the TV.

'Yeah, I am. You want a go?' He pauses it and hands me the controller. He doesn't look at me in the eyes. He rarely does.

'My hands are dirty. You're better than me anyway.'

'Ok.' He goes back to playing. The phone starts ringing and we both ignore it.

'Where's your Mum?'

'Upstairs somewhere. I haven't seen her in a while.'

'Ok. See you in a bit.' I kiss his hair and step up the stairs slowly. My feet: lift heavy, lift heavy, lift heavy. At the top of the stairs I shout a hello to Sarah. She shouts a 'hello' and a 'you alright?' back. I shout 'yeah'.

In our room I pull a towel off the rack and a pair of pants out of the drawer. In the bathroom I piss, hitting the seat and the inside of the lid. The head of my dick is covered in bits of cotton. I flick the blue fluff off. The new pants do this for some reason. I wipe the seat with toilet roll and flush. I pull my shirt off, drop my trousers and pants and, leaning down, pull my socks off. In the shower, the first blast of cold water stings me. I suck air through my teeth. Then it heats. I turn it up so it burns. I lean my head against the white tiles. The burning lines of water; beating, beating, beating down, cleaning the dirt, sweat and dust away down the black plug-hole.

After showering, I dry my body and put on fresh clothes Sarah has left me in the bedroom. I head back downstairs and hear the tap on in the kitchen. It's Sarah. She's washing her hands, pink nails, long and thin. 'Alright, babe. There's a cup of tea on the table for you,' she says. 'Bit cold now. How's work?'

'Tiring. Ta for this, darling.' I sit at the table, putting my palms around the cup. 'The Boss had me digging this hole all day.'

'Yeah?'

I stir my tea, swirling the brown, metal tinkling inside the cup. Sarah's bent at the oven poking at potatoes. Her bum's sticking out towards me. I can see her skin, the gap between top and jeans. I stop stirring, slide my chair back and move towards her. I get down on my knees and lift her top up a bit. I kiss the skin. Big, open-mouthed kisses. I hear her give a little laugh; something she keeps only for me. I like it.

'What's this for?' she asks.

'Nothing,' I say.

'Really?'

'I just wanted to...'

She wiggles her hips a little. 'Yeah? Wanted to?'

'I don't know. I love you and I kiss you because of that. Just like this.' I blow a big raspberry on her back.

'You fucker. That's it. I'm leaving you now.'

'I'm sorry. I couldn't help it.' I look up at her. For a few minutes the only sound is the bubbling pots and purring oven. 'Sarah?'

'Hmm?'

'You don't mean that?'

'What?'

'About leaving?'

'No, of course not, you wally.'

'Because there's nothing I can do.'

'What are you on about? I'm not leaving you, ok? Why the fuck would I?' She stops, turns and gets down on her knees.

'I ain't on about that. I mean... I don't know... You could disappear. Go, or Harry could. And there'd be nothing I could do.'

'About what?'

'I don't know. I mean just one day it'll all be over.'

The day is over. I lie on my bed staring out at the black sky. The door to the shower unlocks and Sarah steps out. 'Harry's asleep,' she says, rubbing her black hair with a towel. Her body is still wet. 'He's a good kid but he needs to make more effort. Are you listening to me?'

'Harry'll be alright. He's only eleven.'

'No. He has to put the effort in now. I want him to have more possibilities than we had.'

'So do I. You know that.'

'I know,' she says. She lies down beside me, her arms stretched out, one hand resting on my stomach, the other hanging loose off the side of the bed. My belly rises and falls, lifting her arm up and down. I look at her wet belly. Her eyes close.

'You know what he said before he fell asleep?'

'What?' I say.

'He said, "Dad smelt funny today."'

'Really? Do you think I do?'

'No. I know you. I know your smell.'

I feel her eyelids with my fingertips. I lean in to her and kiss her top lip. She pulls her hand out of the air and round my neck. I suck and pull on her bottom lip. My hands slip up her sides and I press my hand under her breast. I feel her nipple harden. She leans her head below my chin and kisses my Adam's apple and her small hands move over the small of my back. My fingers move down her body feeling the soft skin of her thighs. A small puff of breath slips out of her mouth. I press my mouth into hers, she presses back. We lick each other's teeth and gums. I kiss below her belly button, gripping her hand in mine. She pulls me up and kisses my mouth again. I pull my pants down and open her legs with my knee. I slide into her. I feel her; press and push and thrust her. She hangs onto my earlobe with her front teeth. I hear her say 'Love'. I kiss the hair covering the back of her neck. My head is pressed into her shoulder and I smell her wet, clean skin.

It's gone two in the morning. I have to get up for work in four hours. I stick my head in Harry's room. His head is pressed into the pillow. I won't wake him. I step down the stairs, fags in one hand, lighter in the other. I unlock the door and sit on the doorstep. The road is empty, except for a few cars and the postbox. Empty of people and quiet. I pull a fag out, put the brown end in my mouth and light. I suck it, hold it inside me, then breathe out the grey smoke in a thin line. I close my eyes. I drag again. I open my eyes and flick the ash in the flowerpot. Something moves. I look up and notice a brown body. It comes from behind a car wheel. It is coming towards me. Its head bops up and down. The fur is dirty; I can smell it. It steps four-legged. Step step step step. The tail sticks up behind it and the tongue hangs down; wet and red. I look, and the fox looks back.

_POEMS

_I CAN'T START MY JOURNAL YET

If I am to do this properly I must start carefully.
It is alright for Billy Collins to be at ease with his journal,
he has been writing one for years and it has the comfort of an old shoe.
It is companionable and has been tried in the battle of ideas
or worse still, the battle of no ideas.
It has not been found wanting and has earned a place in his way of things
and the right to travel with him everywhere, with a little knife to sharpen
    his pencil
      just so.
I bet he doesn't even carry a rubber. Well, an eraser then, as he's American.

I am nervous of starting off in the wrong way.
I must choose the right sort of little book, suitable for lasting confidences,
not one I might decide is uncomfortable when it is less than quarter full.
Then I would worry about the waste if I had to scrap it so soon.
I would worry about whether anything I had written in it
was worth copying out into a new book.
And where to put it if it wasn't.

I don't often wear a jacket now I am a poet
so my notebook must fit in my trouser pocket
so it mustn't get all scrumbled up at the edges before it is full.
But tiny pads are for the small-minded.

I am sure a real poet would rise above this petty stuff
and create, uninhibited, on old envelopes or Hittite wax tablets.
But perhaps Byron had special blank vellum notebooks
shipped out to Italy by a fast barque, and if it became becalmed
he might have been totally unable to complete Childe Harold.

I think I will worry about the decision some more.
This is not a matter for trial and error.

_MY NEW NOTEBOOK

Small
but perfectly formed.
Slim.
Petite even.
With just enough
hint
of black elastic
to inflame the imagination
of a poet.

_DICHOTOMY

'So much depends upon
the damn thing's scanning,'
said the undergraduate,
forsaking his poem
and pilfering a flatmate's plum
from the communal icebox.

So sweet.

_MISFIT

They came and went, one face for all faces
streaming in with clean lines and compliments,
then smoky wide-eyed antibodies,
drawn by a name that isn't even mine.
Slicked on lips rubbed away
to slurs on dirty sheets
reapplied quick so they'd know my face
If they made it through the night.
Most took the memories and left.
Thousand dollars for a kiss, baby,
fifty cents a soul.

And now they gather and share their stories,
the black-hatted masses shaking a collective head
for the tragic, tragic waste.
See, they think they know why I did it.
Some heady mixture of barbiturates
and decline had taken hold;
white dress killer smile,
those days had gone
and I was nothing without the limelight.

Soon they'll be writing songs about me,
the ultimate comeback kid
immortalised in pink satin,
as if I chose to be this way.
Shame on me for buying the happy ending;
they just cut when everyone's smiling.
But nobody dies in Hollywood, I told myself
as the lights just rolled away.

_ENCOUNTER

Japanese students amble
along the pavement,
grown women
dressed as if for kindergarten;

baby-dolls in knee-high socks,
bunches, bows, *hello kitty* motifs
on satchels slung sideways
across slender shoulders

and me, advancing fast,
huffing towards some customary task.
A flat-footed colossus
with long loping strides.

They dive aside,
these pocket-sized Lolitas,
a bonsai tableau rustling in the gust
of the slip-stream as I whoosh past.

Thankyou, I boom.
Aah, they reply.

_THE VIGIL

After two hours of burning, I get dressed
and smoke.

Past the mirror
where your eyebrows push together in the middle
and are deflected up like opposing magnets

wooden toed, tired
sun like a showerhead
shoe-filled bed.

Cut cut cut.
The bright dust has left no company
but doors in parallel lines
like benign nurses.

I crave curves and blurs.
I examine my fingernails,
tomorrow in six hours.
Tonight was bad like a fruit.

jen kahawatte___96___arwen bird

_REFRACTION

A crystal, a plain glass mountain
Let the light shine through
No shadow, just
A rainbow
▽

△
A rainbow
No shadow, just
Let the light shine through
A crystal, a plain glass mountain

_THE FIRE BIRD

She dances, arms raised
in a pool of yellow light,
each finger delicately poised
down to the tiny foot
on which she seems
to stand momentarily
on air, as she dances on points.

A turbaned figure kneels stage left,
hand resting on his silent lute,
twilit, grey, shadowy,
his eyes on her.
In a poor light you could miss him.

The Fire Bird,
a living flame
flickers on the dim green stage
alone with her silent watcher.

The artist must have viewed her
from the dark of Gallery or Stalls,
carried the bright image live,
transferring Diaghilev's art
from stage to canvas in his studio:
a symphony
in yellow, green and grey,
Stravinsky's score echoing as he worked,
the dancer's perfect movements
never quite touching earth.

_AFTER THE FIRE AT MATALAN

Men in uniform lift and lower the tape
for other men in uniform
as the crane rises and circles.
Neighbouring stores close, choked by the acrid plumes,
bank holiday shoppers deprived of DIY and carpets.

And those of us housebound by the flames
walk by late afternoon to view the carcass
of this giant industrial bird, its curved bones
bared like a half-carved turkey,
and inhale charred remains that float
then settle on the concrete of the retail park,
ochre insulation like discarded nesting.

Close to Christmas,
graffiti-ed hoardings disguise the deconstruction,
apologise for the inconvenience, while skip lorries
rattle the ashes of the pyre through the town.
Viewed through the square link fence,
an open space, a pile of rubble.

And still stray slices of the old bird's nest
skim the car park, perch on the branches of the winter trees.

_MISSED YOU ON THE DAY IT RAINED

On the first day
you lashed poles to poles,
vertical and horizontal,

created your own first floor with wooden planks,
filled in the cracks
in the brickwork.

You picked out the flowers and tendrils
on the lintels,
gold on brown,

and now you are painting the pillars
between the windows,
the rounded plinth

a rich chocolate, the column cream,
topped with the curves
of the fleur de lis.

I am learning the exact length and breadth
of the naked patch at the back of your head,
how it shines in the afternoon sun,

the way stray strands arch over
in the breeze
like a field of ripening corn.

If you would only turn round
you could see into my house.

Missed you on the day it rained.

_BLANKET

You only had one pair,
and the devil makes work,
so you scrubbed, swept, polished,
baked in every inch of oven space,
rustled up stews and soups from scraps,
ripped stockings into strips, strapped
beans to poles, fruit to canes,

and by night you circled the square,
unravelled remnants of outgrown woollens
from long-forgotten photos –
shell-pink, peppermint, red-flecked beige –
hooked warmth into the holes,
edged it with a ribbed row of rust.

The ends still dangle: bitten, burnt,
sealed with a sliver of soap.

_STRIPPED

Naked, we step into the shower. I help you manoeuvre the sliding
        door, shuffle
under an incontinent spray. Eyes shut, screwed up tight, you grip my hip
with your good hand, the other rests limp at your side. I shampoo
        your head,
rinse flecks of foam from your face.

A hernia scar, stretch marks, varicose veins, several moles (inspect
        regularly
for changes in colour or size) and greying pubic hair.
Emperor's Gate SW7, 1971 – you always sat at the tap end.

_IF PIGS COULD FLY

If only pigs could fly,
I heard her cry,
and they don't, I know,
I'd change this plastic spit-pot
for a glass of gooseberry wine.
I'd take you back to the garden,
the daffodils, the oak tree,
that seat by the seedless vine.

I'd eat your broad beans in the summer
bottling fruit and making jam.
I'd watch you with our Kitty's kiddy
picking raspberries near the potting shed.

This stinking ward
I'd turn to meadow
with clover, vetch and feverfew
then lord and lady we'd roll in mint, and dance
to the tune of the cuckoo pint.

I'd store you apples,
wrap your wounds with lint,
forget your grumps and grumbles,
moaning moments,
slurs and tumbles.

For if only pigs could fly,
I heard her cry,
I'd do it all again,
I'd stake my claim
despite the nettles' sting
and jump right through
our wedding ring.

_FORENSICS

Watching her sleep, he wondered –

if she should die tonight and yet
remain here till her flesh dissolved
and then be found upon some future wasteland

could the nest of bones
construe her life

the metacarpals
fallen back, as if her grasp
were loosening on some precious thing,

the vertebrae collapsing
as her skull tipped slowly off
the pillow
and the playful
skewing of one femur on the other?

Would they conjecture
from the clustering tarsals how her instep
cradled her heel?
And every shred
of evidence appraised, would they deduce
how recklessly she slept
how not a thought
had come to her of danger – how he shielded
her from harm
at least as much
as human flesh was able?

_ON YOUR DEATH

What a pale business it is. Not dark
nor dramatic nor something
to remember. Just weather
filled with endless rain. And a house
which tumbles for a while and waits
as the dull thuds of life return; the first stirrings
of a bleak thing.

_HOUSE

You lived in me
like viruses in a body,
stamping with your feet,
ignoring the creaks,
stealing the power that
ran through my veins.
I felt you breathe.
I felt you leave
in a bad mood.
You'd slam the door and heave a sigh
to be out of there.
You drew around me
with flowers and ornamental paths,
lit up my windows with oriental scarves.
Like an illuminated letter I stood, yours.
You made changes for the better
or so you thought.
Then you boarded up my windows,
barricaded my doors,
made my skin
water-tight like yours.

_IN CHAINS

You said you used to pull the legs off
insects when you were young.

Now it's petals off our love, one
by one. Watch me carefully

and see my expression,
teach me a lesson. Each daisy,

he loves me. Pain.
He loves me not. Hurt.

If I pick some more and
make a chain

you say I'm a sensitive
flower and no one's to

blame, but I look and see
the petals lying all around our

feet and it's too late
to start again.

He loves me not.

_GILLINGHAM

The train left London's
greyness
passing edifices, gloomy,
dormant, sun trapped in their
confines like a caged peacock.
I hadn't expected more of the same.
As we crossed the great river
and passed through
Clapham, Brixton, Wandsworth,
dilapidation, graffiti, waste,
I had visions of
a nomadic bird finally settling,
then the train stopped here
at Gillingham.
I stare out of the window as if I could
see you but I don't even know your
address, just that you live
here.
And you –
as colourful as a Chagall window
and as soft as an insect's wings,
can you see me?

The train pulls out and
as I look back my eyes can't focus
but I feel my heart quicken.

_A MEMORIAL IN BERLIN

I've come here as a collector
of photographs, not art as far as I'm aware.
I, an insatiable tourist, have come
to this edge almost incidentally.

Walk through
massive grey slabs of concrete,
mute.
Clad in the white of one reluctant winter's
first admission of snow – cold, ephemeral.
Freshly coated confession

deadens the sound
of crunching footsteps, my own.

No names, no dates, no photographs –

No need.

Snap.

In the end
I, at least, can see my way home.

_DAY AND NIGHT

The moon hangs low and dirty yellow, hovering over the thought junkyard like a poxied lover.

In the shrine cities the bombs are very beautiful. They kidnap and militia. There's a humanitarian crisis. What a small word crisis is.

A suspected leftist is stopped. He's a poet and closer to what's right. They'll gun-butt his ribcage till there's something good on television.

A woman runs silently through the streets. Her naked bloodied baby in arms.

The stain seeps into the molecules that prefer to resist. Resist.

_FAITH

If we wear exactly as the next, hat boots storm and troop, then we're united. The M I've carved into the leather of my leg is barely perceptible – only a spy would find it there, perhaps a sniper. It doesn't matter so much that you'd rather be fucking yesterday and the smell of the barn, many of us have similar yearnings – it matters that you refuse to wear the hat with strap that keeps chin firmly in place and thoughts under cover.

_ADVENT 2006

As I applied moisturiser this morning
the newscaster detailed the 56 dead,
200 wounded by a suicide
bomber in Iraq:
day-labourers.
The bomber called them to the car
to kill them.

As I put on eye-shadow
I was wondering about
their families –
but I didn't really have the time because
he was already confirming the
number of prostitutes murdered in
Suffolk now as 5.

I was applying mascara
and starting to think of the murdered girls,
but I didn't have time because
he'd moved on to the murder of a man
outside the police station in Henley –
(good heavens, even Henley –
but it probably isn't manned).

I just had time for some lip-liner
before driving – carefully –
to my appointment,
repetitively praying
to the God I don't believe in:
'Keep us both safe,
please keep us safe.'

And I tried not to think
about the others
who cried
for the money they wouldn't get
and the food they didn't have
and the children who wouldn't eat
and the warmth in the night
they wouldn't hold.

_BLACKOUT, 1942

My thoughts spin like a gyroscope,
a whirl of images returns with flash,
confusing crash of glass, incendiary flares.
The searchlight beams criss-cross, conduct
the earthly siren's wail and whistle blasts.

Next frame, steel wheels spin, slip then grip,
steam spills as carriages chitter-chatter.
Brown labels on lapels, gas masks in hand,
evacuees squashed tight and counted twice.
The journey's long and Granny waits.

Now feather bed, wood smoke and stone flag floors.
Black pudding is a treat but black
on a sleeve denotes a loved one lost. Our shelter is
an apple store. At night, gas lights create ghostly
wall shapes. I borrow boots to fetch the milk.

It's June, bagpipes play and colours fly
as kilted soldiers march toward the train.
Hands wave. They seem so brave but Grandpa says
in war men die. I salute the ones I know.
The Colonel winks at me. He sent a card – just one.

_ARMCHAIR ACTIVIST

See light fall on Che's beret
as it slices through the blinds,
peppered into segments
on the khaki of my chest

his beard full of dapples,
grey hairs he'll never grow
punctures that were echoes
from his best.

The red stars on my T-shirt
act up as hero's wounds –
shiny-sticky ink,
blooded pools

silk-screened neat and tidy,
designed as if by rules,
though ribs were cracked random
and skin shattered through.

And I wear this REVOLUTION word
as though it could ever be
hoping fashion one day becomes
The Truth.

Then I nod into the mirror
at Guevara all in black
and piss away a latte
underneath my listed roof.

_THE F WORD

I wanted to say fuck when I was younger
And I wanted to smash glass and build fires.
And I wanted to run hard and fast across grass and busy roads.
And I wanted to eat and eat and eat butter-covered corn on the cob.

I wanted the games that needed batteries,
And I wanted a gang and a nickname and a knife
And a reputation and spray-painted signs of my existence
And a fast bike.

I wanted love bites and the press of teeth and tongues,
I wanted to put my hand inside girls' damp knickers,
I wanted to smoke and act cool
And press my hardness against any part of them.

I wanted to wear jeans and leather
And things with studs in.
I wanted an earring and tattoos
And scars and scabs and bruises
And all the stories that go with those things.

But most of all I wanted to say fuck when I was younger.

_ANVIL

Are you there, beast of burden
or is that a hole in the world?

You are marked out by your bruises
and betrayed by the playing lamps.
Your hide has suffered
                            (like my forebears, I too
                            am a pugilist)
                    beneath the raping raptures
                    of creation.

and all the while
you sing and have sung
as we build our empires

and our shouts fly
from your one black knuckle.

_MY BEAUTIFUL GREEN IGUANA

Bessie at number 10 has a cat,
a long-haired tom, but I didn't want one.
The cat can't be trusted, even when he's purring.
He may be furry, but he's also barbed
in tongue and in claw.

Not like my gentle green iguana
who pads up arms, balances on shoulders,
and knows all kinds of useful information
about the weather – can measure the humidity
in one swift flick of his delicate tongue.

Some say that cats are godlike creatures
worshipped by the ancient Egyptians.
More fool them! But Bessie's no better.
You should see how she dotes. That cat's
as fat as butter. One time I showed her

my iguana's third eye, hidden within
the roof of his head, scanning the sky.
Clever, that! Not like that puffed-up ball
of fluff at number 10. Who needs all that fur?
Everyone knows bare skin

increases sensitivity. A pet is a friend,
a kindred spirit, not a cuddly toy. My green
iguana has spines that stand up at the nape
of his neck. The skin beneath them boils
in a riot of sympathetic colour.

_IF WE

If we hadn't turned left, if we hadn't filled our mouths with ripe figs plucked from the tree which leant over the wall and into our path, if we hadn't picked up the ball and then thrown it (and you hadn't bounded and smiled), if you hadn't smiled back. You with your dark eyes and your creamy pelt, sticking to us like a guilty conscience. Look at you now, your well-fed belly on the grass, rolling to the left like a sultan!

The lines of the sun are curving over my favourite field.

If in the warm wind you hadn't flung yourself at the blue clumped grass and the wet leaves, haunches thudding, every happy parabola drawing us in tighter than the chain we found around your neck, the chain which made a hard pink patch in the soft folds under your throat

This time tomorrow you'll need to smile at someone else because we'll have packed up and gone.

_FLOTSAM

They did this for us, dashing around Fenwicks
after work with a wedding list which we arranged
in rooms, understanding the relationship between
wall frames and soft furnishings until our own time
came to rush flat out, hand in hand, to family affairs
fixing kids in car-parks, carrying cameras.

And one day on a train or in an airport you stand
by a window saying, 'I can't go on,' and
the next scene you sit down, being reasonable
and somebody stares in disbelief, a child, a wife
and the walls and chairs become flotsam but you
will keep a few photographs, a box of letters.

And friends will say 'It's better to move on
into the Caribbean or the sunlit sea,'
but you will be carrying ingrained the rigid lines
round your eyes, the way you walk and the belief
that moving on now may not be the right thing
unless into the tradition of documenting grief.

_RED TRAIN

Arrow on line
the red train unravels us
as it would unravel a string
and there at its centre
was a man playing
and singing.

Backwards through the dark
on the empty platform
we catch him carrying on
completing the song for us
after the train has gone.

_BIOGRAPHICAL NOTES

Fran Addison, a part-time student and full-time administrator, wrote these poems in response to the module Narratives from Life. She has completed the Diploma in English Literature and Creative Writing and hopes to come up with enough ideas to carry her through the final two years.

Jacqueline Bentley is a psychotherapist in private practice and has just completed the first year of the MA in Creative Writing.

Nicola Berge graduated this year with a degree in English and American Literature and Creative Writing. She hopes to start a career teaching English at secondary school. She saw the year 2007 in when she was visiting a friend in Hong Kong.

Arwen Bird is currently in her first year of studying English and American Literature and Creative Writing. She was born in the north, raised in the south, raves in the Capital and rests in happy Canterbury.

Laura Bottomley has just completed a degree in English and American Literature and Creative Writing. She has applied for a travel-writing MA at Kingston University which she hopes will lead to a career in writing and teaching. Since finishing at Kent she has been working in a nursing home, an experience she has found to be both creatively inspiring and emotionally rewarding.

Isabel Clift is in her third year, studying English and American Literature with Creative Writing. Her favourite writers are J. D. Salinger and Roald Dahl.

Richard Codd graduated in 2007 with a First in English and American Literature and Creative Writing. He is currently juggling earning some money and writing a novel about the city and its shadows.

Susan Cowling is a postgraduate student at Kent, having already studied for her first degree there. She has been published in *Night Train* before and plans to keep writing for ever.

Kay Dawson began her long association with the University of Kent in 1977, arriving at a then stark and treeless campus to embark on an English Literature degree. More recently she has just completed her MA in Creative Writing. She has enjoyed her time here tremendously and is bereft at the thought she will no longer be around, not least to monitor Eliot's relentless slippage down the hill.

Kay Donaghay has recently graduated this year with a degree in English Literature and Creative Writing. Now unable to kick the writing habit, she plans to continue as a post-graduate student in the School of English and start writing a novel.

Graham English wrote 'Jackanory' whilst studying on the English and American Literature and Creative Writing BA. Nowadays, with yet more excellent help, this time on the Contemporary Novel MA, he is writing *Missing People*. Other stories by him have appeared in *Night Train 4* and Comma Press's *Parenthesis* anthology.

Alice Furse was born and grew up in Gillingham. She has just graduated with a degree in English and American Literature and Creative Writing. She currently shares a flat in Brighton with a wookie, and is attempting to write a novel.

Emma Glass is currently studying for her degree in English and American Literature and Creative Writing.

Rebecca Green has recently graduated with a degree in English and American Literature and Creative Writing.

Patricia Griffin is just beginning her final year of a part-time degree in English Literature and Creative Writing. She particularly enjoys writing poetry and has twice been short-listed for the University's T.S.Eliot competition, and published in *Logos* and *Night Train*. Her other passions in life are walking and gardening, activities which allow her to meditate on the years lived in other countries.

Tim Harding is in his second year of studying English and Creative Writing at Kent. He has sort of written one and a half novels and many short stories. He is great. He is unpublished.

Sarah Heath spent her early childhood in Zambia and started her working life as a biologist. She now works part-time as an administrator in education. She enrolled on the Certificate in Creative Writing at the University in September 2006.

Christopher Hobday has just completed a degree in English and American Literature. He has worked on *Logos*, a creative writing magazine published by the School of English, and is currently the editor of the

Canterbury Poets weblog (www.canterburypoets.blogspot.com). He is currently working on a selection of poetry with Luigi Marchini and Gary Studley.

Roger James is about to start his third year of part-time study in Creative Writing. He has had stories and poems published in Kent and Manchester.

Jen Kahawatte is a student on the part-time Certificate in Creative Writing. She has been a computer programmer/systems analyst and primary school teacher, but has now retired and writes and dances for pleasure.

Frances Knight works (or plays) as a musician specialising in jazz and tango music. She initially attended the Certificate in Creative Writing in 2003, when she won the university's TS Eliot poetry prize. She is now studying part time for an MA.

Maria McCarthy is a student on the MA in Creative Writing. Her work has appeared in *Urban Fox* anthologies and in *The Frogmore Papers*. She has written and broadcast for Radio 4, and has self-published a collection of prose and poetry, *Learning to be English*. She has recently taken up the dangerous sport of open mic poetry in the Medway Towns.

Adam McWalters came to UKC as a mature student after taking an access course. He has worked as a software analyst and programmer, living in Islington for a while before becoming disillusioned by city life and worked in the French Alps as a resort manager for 3 winters. He has also travelled Europe in a Camper Van, been the general manager of a health club and worked in cafés from Soho to Canterbury.

Luigi Marchini has just completed his final year of his degree in English Literature and Creative Writing (Part-time) – six years! He won the Canterbury Writers Poetry Prize in 2006 for one of his poems.

Sam Oborne has had fiction published in *Litro*, *Pen Pusher* and *Random Acts of Writing*, as well as on the websites nthposition.com and eastoftheweb.com. He is currently working on a novel and a number of short stories. He lives in Kent with his wife and two rats. Their website is lesobornes.blogspot.com.

Yvette Peden grew up in Australia with sunburn and Skippy. She now lives in a village near Canterbury with her two daughters. She is in the final phase of the MA Creative Writing course

Sharon Petts has been writing seriously for six years and is enrolled on a part-time MA in Creative Writing at Kent. She has completed a Science Fiction novel, which she is touting round to anyone who will look at it, and she is working on a novel for young adults. She is married with two teenage sons.

Stephen Pursey is a student on the MA in Creative Writing. He still doesn't know what a biographical note is. He's 22, enjoys nights out and nights in, and isn't sure how his story will look when it's printed.

Angie Pyman started to write on the University's Certificate in Creative Writing programme, after which she took a year to study at the University of Warwick. She is now back at Canterbury, on the MA programme. She has been working on a novel for just over a year, but finds poetry more suited to her unpredictable life!

Frances Rae has completed her MA at Kent, having begun the Certificate course in Creative Writing in Tonbridge nine years ago. She is in the course of writing a novel.

Martine Ratcliffe is just about to complete an MA in Creative Writing at the University of Kent. She is married with six children and lives in Tunbridge Wells.

Mary Rose Rawlinson had no idea when she started on a two year part-time Certificate in Creative Writing that she would continue for six years. She has just graduated with a degree in English Literature and Creative Writing. It has been a wonderful experience for her and she has learnt so much. She had spent most of her adult life steeped in amateur dramatics and with an avid interest in the professional theatre.

Keith Reyner is a retired Group Captain (RAF) who has just completed his BA in History and Philosophy of Art this year. He is now in his final year for a second BA in Literature and Creative Writing. He and his wife live locally and he has been attending the University as a part-time student for 5 years.

Natalie Savage has just completed a degree in English Literature and Creative Writing after six long years of study at Kent. She intends to finish her novel, but for now wishes to reclaim her life; has joined a gym and plans to learn both Italian and British sign language.

Beverley Smith is currently studying on the Diploma in English and American Literature and Creative Writing. She is involved in the

University Creative Writing Group 'Save As' and has been involved with editing the university writing magazine, *Logos*. She has had short stories published in several magazines and been shortlisted for competitions.

Susan Smith is a retired primary school teacher, studying Creative Writing part-time. Her particular interest lies in both reading and writing poetry, and she loves the concentration and absorption involved in the use of language.

Eric Spreng is still reflecting upon the rich experiences that doing an exchange in Canterbury afforded him. Meanwhile, he is wrapping up his BA in Applied Linguistics at Indiana University. His poems have been published in *Confluence* literary magazine and he was short-listed for the University of Kent's T.S.Eliot prize in 2007.

Gary Studley is the winner of the University's 2007 T.S.Eliot Prize. He is currently in his final year of the part-time BA in English and American Literature and Creative Writing.

Paul Sweeten graduated in English Literature and Creative Writing after three unforgettable years. He'd like everyone to know he works for the RSC, but he must first fill in an application and then perhaps attend an interview.

Helen Ticehurst is a full-time student now in the third year of her degree in English Literature and Creative Writing. She grew up in Brighton and never likes to be too far from the sea.

John Trelawny arrived late at university, coming as he did from the days when only a small minority (5%?) took degrees, and those were mainly vocational. His time at Kent has been a welcome and enjoyable experience after a career which eventually led to the chairmanship of a major British management consultancy.